"Really. I much prefer a Japanese place, Ishida-san," he smiled at her, not hiding the look of admiration he aimed at the V of her blouse. The housing agent blushed under her makeup.

"I imagine I shall just have to sleep in the street. Or else perhaps go back to America." He breathed on the nape of her neck. An imperceptible shiver coursed through her skin. He leaned forward again, as if to examine the listing. Expensive, but the fun would bear it. His lips were very close to her skin now. It smelled sweet and sharp, slightly sweaty. Not at all like the girls he had known, whose white skins smelled somewhat rancid after a day in the heat. She shivered more perceptibly this time, then said "Perhaps we should go and see it. It is unoccupied. My associate is out . . . I can lock up the office for a while."

Other books by Blue Moon Authors

RICHARD MANTON

DREAM BOAT

LA VIE PARISIENNE

SWEET DREAMS

LOVE LESSONS

BELLE SAUVAGE

PEARLS OF THE ORIENT

BOMBAY BOUND

DANIEL VIAN

BLUE TANGO

SABINE

CAROUSEL

ADAGIO

BERLIN 1923

AKAHIGE NAMBAN

CHRYSANTHEMUM, ROSE, AND THE SAMURAI

SHOGUN'S AGENTS

WOMEN OF THE MOUNTAIN

WARRIORS OF THE TOWN

WOMEN OF GION

BLUE MOON BOOKS
61 Fourth Avenue
New York, New York 10003

New Tempo

TOKYO STORY

Akahige Namban

BLUE MOON BOOKS, INC. NEW YORK

First Blue Moon Edition 1990
First Printing 1990

ISBN 0-929654-32-3

Manufactured in the United States of America
Published by Blue Moon Books, Inc.
61 Fourth Avenue
New York, New York 10003

CHAPTER 1:
The *Gaijin* Cometh

Early fall. Tokyo. Clear blue skies and from the tall buildings in Shinjuku one can sometimes see the perfect snow-tipped cone of Mt. Fuji. Andy's feet were sore and his temper foul. Three days of trudging around the town, looking for a place to live, had dampened his enthusiasm for his return to Japan. He had chosen the area for his search with care. Within reasonable distance of downtown and the Marunouchi financial district. Aoyama was too classy and foreign. Shibuya, which he liked, too noisy. Somewhere in between. Not too far from Aoyama Gakuin University with all its pretty coeds was just right. Price was not a problem, despite the stiff "key money," deposit, agent's fee, and "houseowners present" that were necessary for renting a place in Japan. His trust was stingy on some things but would pay for accommodation. He often wondered if he should pad the bill, but he had to learn to live within his means. Fledgling financial consultants should be able to manage their own financial affairs.

Japanese were loath to let apartments to *gaijin:* foreigners. Foreigners ruined the *tatami* mats by walking on them with their street shoes. They didn't know the proper procedures for greeting the neighbors and they inevitably had noisy parties late into the night. Thus the sore feet. There were foreign-type apartments to let, but he was getting more and more insistent about having a Japanese-style home for his new life. Andy felt he knew all the small alleys and streets in this area of Tokyo. And all the sour-faced housing agents.

The office he was standing before was no exception to the rule: bright and cheerful, sterile. As soon as they heard his request, the polite refusals would start. Andy had to force himself to step inside. He peered through the window first. The usual cards and maps. A woman talking to a man in a business suit.

The man stepped out just as Andy turned in at the door. He was in a hurry but his steps faltered as he saw Andy. Andy was used to the reaction and ignored it. The man cast a sharp look at Andy's face, stopped for a second, seemed to change his mind, then continued on down the street.

Andy looked at the housing agent's flinty face. She had refused several suggestions he had made. The only option for a foreigner in her opinion, was a Western-style apartment. He tried again, to impress her with his familiarity of things Japanese. He thought he could detect a hint of mischievousness, even fun in her. Besides, he liked middle-aged businesswomen. When they let go, all hell was likely to break loose. Experimentally, he moved closer. His warm breath stroked the skin of her arm as he bent forward over the list.

"Perhaps this one?" he asked tentatively, pointing to one of the addresses at random.

"Oh no, Middler-san, that would never do. Very very expensive I'm afraid."

He looked at her face. Smooth round contours with a perfect skin greatly hampered by heavy makeup. Hair in a high hairdo. Severe clothes and rather thick ankles and calves. About forty years old. He shrugged: Where one technique did not work, another must serve. This was his second week in Tokyo and he was getting desperate.

He stood very close to her, crowding her personal space as much as he dared. He fumbled in his jacket with one hand while pointing out possibilities with another, being careful to slide the skin of his hard arm across her hand as often as possible. As he produced his letter of introduction, he let his wallet fall. Her eyes widened at the bulging leather case. It was not unusual for individuals to carry around large amounts of money, but *gaijin* rarely did. It was also all of his cash.

He moved to the wall map. The houses to let were coded. He pointed again at the place that had caught his fancy. It was a fairly new apartment house, three bedrooms and a large main room. A Japanese bath. A very large place by Japanese standards.

"Why don't we go and see that one?" he asked.

"But Middler-san, surely you would prefer a western place?"

He laid his hand on her shoulder lightly to emphasize his words. She turned her face, startled at the uncommon gesture.

"Really. I much prefer a Japanese place, Ishida-san," he smiled at her, not hiding the look of admiration he aimed at the V of her blouse. The housing agent blushed under her makeup.

"I imagine I shall just have to sleep in the street. Or else perhaps go back to America." He breathed on the nape of her neck. An imperceptible shiver coursed through her skin. He leaned forward again, as if to examine the listing. Expensive, but the fund would bear it. His lips were very close to her skin now. It smelled sweet and sharp, slightly sweaty. Not at all like the girls he had known, whose white skins smelled somewhat rancid after a day in the heat. She shivered more perceptibly this time, then said "Perhaps we should go and see it. It is unoccupied. My associate is out . . . I can lock up the office for a while."

The apartment was everything he could have expected. A bit large for his needs, but airy and pleasant. It was in a newly built apartment building fronting onto a *shoten gai,* a shopping street lined with small shops and businesses. Not too far away was the hum of the Omote Sando area and the main street from Shibuya to the center of Tokyo. Ishida-san, the agent, stood on stockinged feet while he made his inspection. The telephone rang.

"Probably my office," she said. "My business partner." She talked quietly into the mouthpiece, following Andy with her eyes while he wandered about the place.

She rejoined him. "You see, Middler-san. Completely unsuitable. I am sure I can find you a nice Western-style apartment."

"Not at all," Andy smiled, trying to show enough confidence to convince her. "This one suits me just fine. Thank you for showing it to me." He stepped deliberately into her personal space and touched her hand. "I'll take it."

"But it is quite unsuitable," she said.

She walked across the room into the hallway area and he followed. To indicate indifference, she looked into the mirror hanging on the wall. Before it was a tall bureau, abandoned or perhaps forgotten by the previous occupant. She laid her bag on the bureau, extracted her compact, and started applying powder to her face. She was ready to go Andy noted. A brief blaze of anger was followed by detached amusement. She would not get rid of him so easily. He walked up beside her, staring into the mirror at her. After examining his determined face, she turned back to her own.

"You have beautiful taste," he said, peering over her shoulder.

She started to say the proper formal phrases of denial, and he raised one hand, as if to move her hair out of the way of his sight.

"I used to be a fashion photographer. Few women have bones like yours." Her harsh expression softened somewhat. He tilted her head, gently, to one side, then another. "Have you tried a lighter shade?" he asked, noting her lipstick. "Oh, I am sorry. I'm bothering you," he added as an afterthought. His hands were at the nape of her neck now, exploring with light feathery touches. Her lips firmed and for one moment he thought she would turn to go. The light touch increased slightly as he asked "Have you been photographed?"

This time she giggled. "Me? At my age?"

"Surely when you were younger? Besides, a mature woman, particularly one with your skin and bone structure, really photographs much better."

She stared into the mirror and saw his face descend to the side of her neck. Her eyes widened but she made no attempt to pull away. He massaged the side of her neck and his lips nibbled at her nape—that part of a woman which is, as traditional belief had it, the most erotic of all. Andy smiled and pressed his body forward slightly.

His palms rested lightly on her shoulders as if to move her aside. Under his hands her shoulders were slight but firm. Her buttocks pressed against him and she noted the erection poking into the small of her back. He exerted the tiniest amount of pressure and she slid gracefully to her knees. He lowered himself beside her and kissed her neck. She turned her head modestly and he licked softly at her nape. She gave an involuntary shudder. It was accompanied by a softening of her body, as if she were nestling into his arms.

One hand slid to her small flat breast. His chest pushed her forward, and she leaned against the bath. With his other hand he undid his fly. His cock sprang into the air, pushing against her skirt. She braced herself neither helping nor hindering his actions.

Andy raised her skirt until his stiff horn could slip under.

He moved her panties aside. The tight band constricted his movements and scraped his cock, but he was too aroused to care. He probed about for a moment. She moved protestingly as his cock nosed at her anus, then subsided as he found the right target. He shuffled slightly forward and his cock entered slowly into her. Andy continued licking the nape of her neck, and she uttered a long drawn out moan. Once seated inside her, he started moving back and forth. She was raised almost on tiptoe by the difference in their heights and she sagged with relief against him as he entered her at full length. He explored her leisurely with his hands. He tweaked her nipples, then stroked her rounded stomach. She undid her blouse to help his exploration. The hard thrust of his penis into her brought her sharp hips up to meet his. They gasped together. His movements speeded up as did the pace of her moans. At last she raised her head, eyes closed. He bit her neck as gently as he was able. She drove herself mercilessly against him, aided by his probing fingers on her erect clitoris.

She turned a moment in his arms, examining his softening penis shyly, as he tucked it away. Andy stroked her cheek lightly and said "It is a wonderful apartment and I will take good care of it."

Ishida smiled roguishly as she adjusted her clothing.

"Middler-san, I must come and examine the house from time to time. . . ."

"Please do so. You should also check if all the equipment is in working order. . . ." He grinned at her and she giggled behind her hand.

It took Andy two hours to get the money from his bank and sign the papers. The house was owned by a company rather than an individual, and so there were few of the social civilities so important to doing business in Japan. Towards evening he turned the key in the door and stepped inside.

He froze as he was removing his shoes. There was another pair at the street level of the entrance. And sounds within the apartment. He started to straighten up as he heard steps, and a tall young man, pale-faced but obviously Japanese, stood before him, looking at Andy's face questioningly.

"Yes?" said the stranger. "What can I do for you?" He spoke English with a California accent.

"What are you doing in my apartment?" asked Andy.

"I was about to ask you the same thing," said the stranger. "I just rented it this afternoon."

CHAPTER 2:
Police Report

"Someone played a trick on us," Jim said after they woke early in the morning. Andy said nothing as he set about making coffee. They eyed one another suspiciously. Both had been too tired to do much talking on the previous evening, beyond almost monosyllabic civilities. It had been too late to call up their respective landlords' agents.

Outside, the rumble of trucks on the main street could be barely heard.

"We've got to settle this."

Andy nodded over his cup. His head was beginning to clear as the liquid dispelled the early morning fog. "I can't understand it. This is the first time I've heard of an owner going to two housing agents at the same time. At least in Japan."

"Probably just trying to ensure a rental."

"Yeah, but you don't do things like that in Japan."

"There's something weird about it," Jim said.

"Who knows what evil lurks in the hearts of men?" Andy asked, grinning.

"He he he, Only the Shadow knows!" Jim completed the

slogan. "Hey, how did you know that one?" They both laughed.

"Truth to tell, this place is a little big for one . . ."

"I was about to suggest the same thing," said Jim. "Any particular vices?" he asked cautiously.

Andy looked at him for a long minute. "Only two. Insatiable curiosity. And women."

"Hey, me too. At least the second. Why the curiosity, though?"

"I just gotta know what's going on. What about you?"

"Drink. Gambling. Highlife. And women. Lots of the latter."

"Should have had it off with the housing agent then . . ." Jim cocked his head. "Don't tell me you . . . ?"

Andy grinned and winked. "Yep."

"Now I understand how they managed to rent it to two guys at once. . . . . Shake, partner."

They shook hands with mock solemnity.

"There's one thing that bothers me though," said Jim. "Your face."

Andy started to scowl. He was sensitive about his appearance. Brown hair streaked with dark blond, brown eyes, dark skin with a prominent hooked nose. Armenians, Indians, Jews, all took him for their own. Growing up in a household of tow-headed blue-eyed children had not done his confidence any good either. Even being told he was adopted had not eased his feeling of alienation.

"No, I mean I've seen your face before. Somewhere . . ."

Andy cast his mind back and looked at Jim, trying to imagine him as he might have looked years before. "There is something about your face, but I can't . . . Nope. Maybe it'll come back. Certainly I've never been to California, and if, as you say you've never left it except to come to Japan . . ." He ran a palm across his chin in perplexity. The rasping reminded him that he needed a shave. That he had an interview, a business to start. "My God, the time!"

Jim stayed with his tea. He would need to buy a computer, to browse through computer catalogs and go to the shops in Akihabara, where the electronics market was.

He was reviewing to himself the various merits of the NEC, Fuji, and IBM computers when he was brought back to reality by Andy's yell from the bathroom. The paler man catapulted into the kitchen and stared at Jim wildly. "Goddamn, Goddamn," was all he could utter.

He grabbed Jim's arm and hauled him to the bathroom. Andy's hand trembled.

"Look at that!" Andy pointed at the mirror. Two faces peered back at them. Jim's turned into a mask as he realized what Andy had seen. Slight differences in hair, color, and size aside, the two faces were the same.

"Fucking hell," Jim whispered. "It can't be."

"But you're Japanese!" Andy whispered. "A *Nisei*. Are you? Well, aren't you?"

"Yes." Jim's voice was unsteady. "My parents were *issei*. But . . . but I was adopted . . ."

They stared at one another.

Andy left, still struggling with his tie. The sight of Jim Suzuki's face in his mirror had upset him more than he could tell. He had resented being told he was adopted. His foster father had not known his parents. Only that his mother was Mary Typhon, who had been unable to raise her child. She had met John Middler through a mutual acquaintance, and John and his wife had agreed to raise the child Andrew for her. There was some money in it. The Middlers were struggling professionals and had been told they had no chance of having children. The latter had proven to be untrue. Medicine had advanced and they had had children. But they had loved

Andy and treated him, even after the birth of their own
children, as their own son. In his more reflective moments
Andy acknowledged his debt, and more importantly his love
for his foster parents. Thinking of the good times, he set forth
towards the subway.

And Jim was puzzled. The Suzukis had been a traditional
farming family in the Napa valley. He had known he was
adopted from the start; it was common practice among Japanese families and no one thought it odd. He had been raised a
Suzuki and a Suzuki he had remained, even when going away
to college. A pleasant surprise—a fund that paid his way—
had kept him in school. He was now working lazily on his
doctorate in systems analysis, in no hurry to leave school.

His musings were interrupted by the doorbell. He opened,
saw the official uniform, and swallowed hard. Then realizing
his pot-smoking days were far behind him, he managed to
relax. It was also incorrect to think of the official figure before
him as a policeman. Policewoman was more accurate.

She looked even more surprised than he. She bowed slightly
and then said "I am from the *koban,* the police post of the
neighborhood. We are having an anti-crime campaign. We have
also reports of a man lurking about the neighborhood." Her
English was heavily accented but comprehensible.

"That is probably my friend," said Jim politely. "A *gaijin?*"

"No, Japanese. No doubt our alertness has scared him
off," she said. She stood straight before Jim in her grey-blue
uniform. Her figure was chunky and her calves and ankles
thick. She looked almost crosseyed, peering up at him from
under heavy dark lashes and the ridiculous little pillbox hat.

Jim smiled. It was never a good idea to annoy the police.
Besides, she looked rather cute.

"Won't you come in and explain?"

"Oh no, I do not want to bother. We have a display of
locks. For your apartment. This is not so good." She indi-

cated the knob lock. "There are many bad people about. Many burglaries."

"It's not so bad," he said, thinking of life in big city USA. The average Japanese cop would have been horrified. A crime wave in Japan consisted of ten burglaries a day throughout the twelve million population of Tokyo. "Won't you come in?"

"No, I must not. Also,"—her "L" came out sounding like an "R" and she fished in her large purse,—"can you please fill out these?" She handed him pink neighborhood registration slips.

Jim bowed slightly and received the slips with two hands, saying "Thank you very much" in Japanese.

"Ah, your Japanese is excellent!" she said admiringly.

"No, not at all," he smiled again, then moved away from the doorway. "Please come in and explain about the campaign. I was on my way to make tea and the kettle is boiling . . ."

Slowly she stepped out of her shoes and up onto the mat surface. She sat down beside the small table and looked around at the room while Jim went to make the tea. When she saw him bringing the tray she rose to her knees and insisted on pouring the tea. Her thick-wristed hands managed to pour the green liquid without spilling a drop.

"You must be an excellent housewife!"

She giggled and hid her mouth with her hand. "But I am not married!!"

"Ah, you should be then! A pretty policewoman like you!"

"Oh no, no one will go with a police!"

"But why not? You are so pretty, you must have a boyfriend!"

She shook her head and giggled again behind her hand.

He laughed and pushed the plate of cakes at her. She took one and placed it on a small plate and handed it to him.

"You should come here everyday! I usually do not eat so elegantly! And you serve so well." The glimmering of an idea took shape in his mind.

"Oh no. I have hands of a farm girl. That's what I am, really: a farm girl from Yamaguchi." She looked down, with sadness.

He took her hand and patted it. She sniffed a couple of times. He stroked her hand gently as a silent tear ran down her cheek. "I'll never get married. I'm too old and no man will want me."

Jim slid over beside her still on his knees. "Nonsense." He stroked her firm erect back. "Any man would see you and note how kind and desirable you are. You must not despair. *I* think you are extremely attractive."

"But I'm a cop! No one want's to kiss a cop!" she sniffed, using the vulgar Japanese term *poliko* for herself.

"No! Not at all!" There was real shock and concern in his voice and she looked at him in surprise. "Why, I would love to kiss you. Here . . ." Jim's lips descended on hers. He applied some pressure and her lips gradually opened as her eyes closed. His right hand crept up to the back of her neck and he massaged the spot under her hairline. Her breathing quickened as his lips parted and his tongue softly licked her full lips. They tasted of lipstick and woman sweat. His tongue penetrated her lips and she sucked at him hungrily. She pulled his head to hers and placed his hand on her breast. Through the heavy layers of fabric Jim could feel the hint of a tumescent nipple. He squeezed and she squealed under his lips.

Then he kissed her neck and his hands went to her waist. The zipper of her skirt was behind her and she had to lean to one side to allow him access. She slumped neatly to the tatami which smelled faintly of new-mown hay. He followed her, his lips at the V of her blouse which had come undone. She was thrusting her hips at him and mumbling incoherently as he lowered the zipper.

He pulled off her skirt and underthings and applied his mouth fully to her mound. She moaned and squirmed on the tatami. Her thick legs clamped about his head. Jim's tongue probed the channel between her lower lips and found it blocked. She moaned and shuddered again as his fingers probed the entrance to her virgin entrance.

He pulled away from her and looked at her sweat-beaded round face for a moment. Her lips were slightly parted, the lipstick smeared.

"Are you brave?" he whispered.

"Yes!" she hissed.

He pressed the full length of his body to her blocky form. She shuddered expectantly. His erection felt tight against her legs. Gently he pried her thick muscular thighs apart. He licked her sweaty tasting lips and his hand slid the length of her rough uniform coat. He guided the head of his swollen prick to the sopping entrance to her cunt. With his left hand he fumbled at the buttons of her blue-gray jacket. She clutched him to her body. The tip of his cock found the mark and he gently twiddled it at the slick portal.

He sought her mouth again, then shoved his hips forward. She cried out softly, but her hands pulled at him as if to hurry up the process. Jim lunged forward, tearing through the thin membrane. She uttered a squeak, part pain, part surprise at the pleasure she felt. He touched their joined parts with silent fingers. His shaft was well embedded in her, and he set about widening the entrance with small movements of his hips. Gradually he sank deeper into her and the volume of her moans increased. When their hairs were joined he stopped moving to allow her vagina to adjust. He raised his body over hers, then led one of her hands to the juncture of their hair. She smiled at him shyly, then urged him on. He started to move in her while at the same time trying to undo the final brass buttons on her coat.

Brushing his hands aside the young policewoman undid her jacket, and then opened her white blouse to his gaze. He fastened hungry lips to her prominent nipples, massaging the fleshy protuberances alternately with his tongue and teeth. She encouraged him by digging her strong fingers into his head, and jogged her rump up to meet his loins.

Soon she was breathing heavily and he started slamming his body violently into hers. She cried out, urging him on with rapid motions of her hands. Jim responded and ground his hips into hers in a circular motion. For a moment she stiffened. Her teeth showed in the rictus of her mounting orgasm, and then she collapsed with a sigh.

He gradually brought his motions to a stop. She smiled up at him. He dipped his head and kissed her, then withdrew his hands from her soft breasts. His hands slid down her body until they rested under her buttocks. They were firm balls of muscle and well-padded flesh. He rolled to one side, then pulled her over on top of him.

"Thank you. At last I can remove my clothes. Otherwise they will get wrinkled and the sergeant will get mad," she explained ingenuously.

"That's not all it's good for," Jim chuckled. He jerked his rump up in the air. His left hand grasped her buttock tightly, while his right diddled the tiny red-stained clitoris that peeped out from the matted thicket of her cunt hairs. Suddenly the advantages of the new position occurred to her. She bent her head, forcing her red mouth onto his, then bit and licked his chest and nipples. Curiously she watched as the shaft of his cock appeared and disappeared into her body. Jim's index finger massaged her rear hole and she giggled as she craned her neck trying to see it at work. Soon they both became serious again, and her movements up and down became more forceful. He pinched and pummeled her buttocks with one hand, while the other roved over her front. At last she gave a grunt and settled her mound firmly against him. He twisted violently, trying to stuff her full of his cock, trying to ram through to her skull. Stars exploded before his eyes with the force of his orgasm. Waves of milky fluid spurted up her channel, the overflow running out along the shaft embedded in her. She sagged gratefully over his chest and he gently stroked her hair and sweat stained back.

She dressed slowly and carefully, regaining the anonymity of her uniform.

"Teraoka-san," he said, noting her badge. "What is your name?"

She smiled a brilliant white-teethed smile. "Michiko."

"Will you come again?" he asked.

"Only to check your residency permit," she teased. "And of course, if you have any reports about the prowler . . ."

He had forgotten completely about the purpose of her visit. "I shall need police protection then . . ."

She turned to leave the room, and an oddly colored ink painting caught her eye. It was lying next to the wall, ready to be hung.

"You like Japanese painting?" she asked.

"Yes," Jim said. "Though this is somewhat unusual. Most people don't care for the style. I find it attractive. It is my roommate's. I have no idea where he got it."

She laughed. "Then you're not so unusual. I've seen such paintings before. A man who had some trouble. His paintings were stolen, all except some in this style. The purples are very distinctive."

"Was he Japanese or *gaijin?*" he asked.

Michiko laughed uneasily. "You know, I don't know. Not

sure. Maybe mixed. Come to think of it, he looked much like
you.''

His interest quickened, but all he said was "Maybe a
relative. What was his name?''

"Kitamura, or Kitahara I think.''

"Ah, from Nerima Ward?''

"No. Someplace in Kita Ward.'' She gave him the address. "You can ask the police box there. They would know
his address. It was three years or so ago that it happened.''

"Ah, that might be my uncle. I've never met him, but I
heard he lived in the area. I should visit him.''

"Well, ask at the Gaigodai stop police post. Goodbye
lover, I must be going.''

She left, now, he noted, with a distinct sway to her hips
rather than a *poliko's* usual clumping.

"Shall we talk about it?'' They were busy arranging their
furniture and hanging paintings and scrolls on the walls.
There were great differences in their preferences and tastes,
but somehow they all seemed to harmonize. Andy was sucking a finger where a sharp picture hanger had pierced the
skin. "OK'' was all he mumbled.

"Family history,'' said Jim. "None. Adopted son of the
staid and hard-working Suzuki family, Issei, of Napa Valley,
California, and Shimogawa-gun, Gumma-ken, Japan. No idea
who my real parents were. My parents took me on as an
obligation to a friend, who was himself obligated to another
friend. Short stint in the military, in Germany, then U. C.
Berkeley. That's it.''

"Nothing odd about that,'' Andy said.

"Only one thing,'' Jim sat on a packing chest. "I never
paid for any schooling. There was a fund . . . Hell, it still
exists since formally I'm a student here. It pays my tuition
and basic living expenses as long as I'm a student.''

"Would it surprise you very much to know I have a similar fund?" asked Andy.

"No." Jim said and looked out the window. "What else?"

"Born to Mary Typhon: unmarried mother, or so I gather. Adopted by the Middler's with her full consent, which I know, having seen the document. Harvard, paid for by our friend the fund, Tokyo U. for two years as a graduate student, back to New York, now research into fiscal economics and trying to set myself up as a financial consultant. That about summarizes it."

"The Suzuki's would never admit that their son is an *ainoko*."

Andy made a face. "I've never liked that word. 'Love child' sounds too much like condescending to the evil Eurasian, which I guess we both are . . ."

"Same date of birth . . . Hey, there's something wrong here. Let's say we're brothers. I assume the thought has occurred to you?" Andy nodded and Jim continued. "Then if Mary Typhon—odd name that—is Japanese, then we both should look Japanese, but we don't. I mean, you look like a *gaijin*. . . ."

"Then maybe we've got a very active father, and two different mothers."

"Yeah, that would account for it. Tell you what, let's see if I can't get some information about these three parents of ours."

"How?"

"Well, we can explore several avenues. One is the fund. I bet it'll turn out to be the same one. You'd best tackle that. Second, I had the neighborhood police here today . . . Oh, by the way, you have to fill in this pink slip." Jim handed over the police registration form. "Anyway, she saw that painting of mine—the one with the swirling purples which I brought from home—and said she knew a man . . ."

"She?" said Andy. "I thought you said policeman?" He grinned.

Unfazed, Jim grinned back. "Actually I said police, not policeman, but in this case you happen to be right. We did, and a fine handful she is . . ."

"I've never laid a policewoman," mused Andy.

"Get your mind back on business," Jim said. "I'll introduce you. Later. She told me there was a man who looked like me—us I suppose—living in Kita ward. It's worth following. I can do that."

"Let's say we do all that, then what?"

"Then nothing. Wouldn't you like to meet your real parents?"

Andy shrugged. "Real? My real parents are in New York. These guys just had a night's fun whose consequence was myself. But, just for fun, ok. There's something else we might look at—the owners of the building. The whole business, renting to both of us. . . ."

CHAPTER 3:
Mahjong as Life

"Do you play Mahjong?"

Andy, who was trying to figure out how the computer worked, looked up. Jim was lounging in the doorway, dressed casually in jeans. "Not very well," Andy said. "I majored in *pachinko*."

"Hey, you're the one who spent time at a Japanese university. Damn, I've got two friends coming over tonight to play."

"No problem," said Andy. "I'm going to be at the library and then I'm going drinking with a friend. We're working on some new figures. How the hell am I supposed to do any work when this goddamn machine won't cooperate . . ." He glared at his computer. Jim grinned and moved to help. Andy appeared to have no mechanical sense whatsoever, and though the benefits of a computer were readily apparent, his ability to master it after two weeks was extremely limited.

Jim opened the door for his friends. Nakabe and Ito were both in computers. Nakabe was a salesman in a large computer shop in Akihabara. He and Jim had gotten friendly while Jim was doing the shopping for Andy and himself. Ito had recently started running his own software consultancy firm and had introduced himself to Jim at the university. Nakabe, Jim knew, was the heir to a large firm in Gifu prefecture in Central Japan. His lowly position at Akihabara was a common practice: an opportunity for the provincial young to work off steam while getting some practical training.

They stepped into the apartment, followed by a pretty girl.

"This is Chieko. She can make drinks for us," Nakabe said.

"Nakamura Chieko," she introduced herself, bowing modestly.

"Suzuki Junichi." Jim bowed in return and invited her in formally. Nakabe, apparently, was playing the typical Japanese male, and simply ignored her.

They seated themselves around the low square table and Jim told them that his roommate would not be there. Ito jerked back from his examination of the room's contents: a mixture of Western and Japanese art, a large stereo cabinet bought second-hand by Andy, central heating. The apartment was magnificent by Japanese standards, and he wondered how Suzuki could afford it.

"We can't play then," Nakabe threw himself on the floor. "I was looking forward to it."

"I'm sorry. My friend had to go out. I thought perhaps, since she is here, that Nakamura-san would play with us."

They looked at one another with some dismay. Mahjong was normally a men's game, but they needed a fourth. Chieko giggled.

"All right, sit down," Nakabe said gruffly. "You know how to play?"

"Of course!" she said indignantly, then giggled again, hiding her mouth behind her hand.

"We're playing seriously here!" Nakabe warned her. "Can

you stand the consequences?'' He made a circle with thumb and finger that meant money.

She shrugged. She had a flat, rather broad face and her hair hung smoothly to her shoulders and was cut in a fringe over her forehead. A small hooked nose and narrow black eyes completed what Jim could see. He wondered if Nakabe had ever been in her, and what she would feel like.

"I'll get some beer," Jim said.

"Oh no, please, allow me," Chieko said. She rose gracefully and went into the kitchen.

"There's some dried squid in the cupboard," Jim called after her. Quietly, he added to Nakabe, "Where did you get her?"

Nakabe grunted, then said "This is only the second time we've been out. I'm going to take her to a movie, and then . . ."

"Then what?" said Ito, leaning forward eagerly.

"Then we'll see," said Nakabe.

"Huh! I bet you've never been in her," Ito said with a grin. His long face twitched.

"Look who's talking!" Nakabe snorted. "I bet you've never been in a woman *at all*. Anyway, shut up . . ."

Chieko returned, balancing a tray with glasses and bottles of beer and a plate. On the plate she had arranged strips of the yellow-white dried squid Jim liked, and some toasted mixed nuts. She had taken the time to arrange the snack in a pleasing pattern. She distributed the glasses and took one for herself.

Jim had reversed the surface of the low table. The bottom, typical in Japan, was covered with green baize. A second, smaller table held the drinks and *otsumami* snacks of salty crackers and nuts. The girl played, but not enthusiastically. She was also busy catering to Nakabe; lighting his cigarette, pouring his beer. The room filled with smoke. Some beer spilled and Chieko hurried to mop it up before it stained the *tatami*.

"Suzuki-san," she called out, "are there any more *otsumami?*"

Jim rose to show her where more of the snack packages were to be found. Chieko looked at his tall figure as he entered the kitchen. She had gone out with Nakabe—tall, handsome, and rich—fully intending to let him have her. Not that she was a virgin. Chieko had experimented frequently with her own body. She had lost the physical evidence of her virginity with her own fingers. She had found that her cunt was extremely expansive. The process had been pleasing and she was ready for more. Nakabe was right, she had thought: young and wealthy enough to give her a good time before and after. Now she regretted her choice a little. Jim was much better looking, notwithstanding the peculiar cast of his features. He brushed against her as he passed in the narrow kitchen, and she swivelled her hips in what she hoped was an invitation.

They returned to the game. The beer and whiskey had made everyone happier. Chieko felt her own inhibitions slipping away. Unfortunately, the drink also lessened her calculating abilities, and by the end of the round she had discovered that she did not have the money necessary to cover the lost points.

She giggled and said to Jim, who had won the round, "I'll have to owe it to you."

"Nope," said Ito. "No IOUs. Against the rules."

She pouted. "Nakabe-san, you pay for me."

The young man looked at her in surprise. "Why?"

She scowled. The drink and the situation made her reckless. She reached to her waist and quickly drew off her sweater. Underneath it she wore a thin, sheer slip. Her nipples showed clearly, black against the white of the slip. She tossed the sweater onto the table.

"I'll pay for my stake with this," she said.

Ito, barely taking his eyes off her breasts said "Well, I don't know . . . It's against the rules . . ."

"Nonsense," said Jim. "I'm the winner of this round and I'm prepared to accept it." He reached forward and collected the sweater. She noticed that his eyes, unlike those of the others, were on her face rather than her breasts. She liked that. It showed control, and appreciation.

They mixed the tiles which clicked with their characteristic sounds.

"Now what?" Nakabe asked her.

"Wouldn't you like to put something up?" Chieko asked, teasing. Only Jim noticed a serious undercurrent to her question.

"I've still got plenty of money left," Nakabe answered.

"I'll put up my trousers," said Ito, more than half drunk. His courage always rose with his alcohol level.

"Phoo, what would we do with your stinking pants?" Nakabe growled. He seemed embarrassed, his face flushed.

Jim said nothing. Chieko looked at him with disappointment. He rose and fiddled with the stereo, then turned up the heating and sat down.

"I'll put up . . . my pantyhose," she said.

They played their tiles, collecting and throwing them away as they tried to make points. Patterns began to emerge as they totalled up the sets. As the tension rose the three men grew flushed. The heat in the room seemed oppressive. Ito loosened his collar. Nakabe took deep gulps of his beer. A tiny streak of sweat ran down between the vale of Chieko's breasts.

Jim smiled at her. "Getting warm, isn't it?"

She smiled back shyly. The implications of his remark struck her and her almond eyes darted to the thermostat on the wall. She smiled again, with gratitude.

They finished the rubber. Chieko and Nakabe had lost.

"Well?" Jim said as he collected the pot.

She stood up and giggled behind her hand again.

"Get it off," Nakabe said.

She reached behind her and raised her calf-length skirt. She fumbled under the skirt, glaring at Nakabe, reached for her tights, then stooped. The filmy undergarment came down her legs. She kicked it off and sat down before the table quickly. The liquor was beginning to wear off, replaced with a rush of apprehension.

"What's your stake now?" Jim said as he poured her a large beer.

She gulped it. The flush returned to her cheeks and she giggled again.

"My . . . my panties!"

"You'll be in trouble if you lose again," Jim winked at her like a fellow conspirator.

"You should try your dress first. Fine stuff. Dresses," Ito said.

They played again.

"Damn, it's hot," muttered Nakabe. Suddenly he rose and stripped off his tie and shirt, remaining in his undershirt.

"Are you losing too?" asked Ito.

"Just hot. Might as well strip off my pants too." He stripped to his shorts. Chieko would have ignored it in the normal course of things. Japanese men often undress, even in public when the weather merits it. But being conscious of her own undress gave her pause. Jim noticed her eyes flicking anxiously in Nakabe's direction.

Jim tried to soothe her. "Well, I knew you wouldn't be the only one to lose all the time."

Nakabe and Ito both found it hard to concentrate. Their eyes darted to Chieko's breasts. Ito leaned back, casually he thought, trying to get a glimpse of her legs. His pose mixed diffidence and aggression.

Chieko ended the round with a small pile of coins before her. Jim smiled and poured some more beer for all of them. She smiled back and sipped her beer in relief. But the next round was a disaster.

Ito stared at the filmy garment before him on the table. She had taken her panties off without rising and put them on the table without any outward expression. Her heart was pounding. Ito grabbed the panties and pressed them to his face. Nakabe, eyes wide, reached for her. Chieko shrank back. Jim grasped his shoulder and restrained him. "Play!" he ordered. Nakabe subsided, though rivulets of sweat ran down his face and his hands twitched.

She was not a good player. There was a hint of frightened triumph as her skirt came off. Her shift reached halfway down her thighs, and Ito bent down to look up at her cunt, his hand playing obviously with the bulge in his crotch. She tried to ignore him, took a deep gulp of her beer, and wagered the slip.

"Well, the only thing left now is yourself," Jim said judiciously. He smiled at her and she held his gaze for a long moment, then smiled slightly in turn. She twisted a long strand of hair over her face and nodded wordlessly. She sat formally on her knees, conscious that Ito and Nakabe who sat on both sides of her were staring openly at the dark patch between her legs, hoping to catch sight of her slit. She was embarrassed, but something lusty was growing, keeping her at her seat. She helped mix the tiles, then slammed her own down into the row in front of her, and concentrated on her play. It surprised her that she did not mind losing at all.

"I've lost," she said dully, but with a hint of satisfaction. She rose from the table followed by three pairs of eyes. Her body was good. Her breasts small and pointed and her hips wide. Ito licked his lips as he saw the triangle of black hair at the base of her gently rounded belly. Nakabe reached for the fly of his underpants.

She laid herself down on the tatami, putting a flat *zabuton* cushion under her buttocks and spreading her legs, feet flat on the floor and knees raised. Her breasts spread on her chest. She turned to look at the men, eyes glazed.

Nakabe and Ito were on their feet with a howl. Nakabe, slightly less drunk and less hampered by clothes reached her first. Ito was struggling with his pants and hopping across the floor at the same time as Nakabe flopped on top of her, his mouth groping for an erect nipple, his hands clawing at the slit between her legs. Ito fell to the floor beside the couple, pulling at Nakabe as he tried to precede him, hardly knowing what he was doing as he groped for some portion of female flesh.

"Stop it! Stop right now!" Jim's face was flushed and his eyes glittered. Nakabe clung grimly to Chieko's breasts, causing her to whimper with fright. Jim grabbed Nakabe roughly by the shoulder and hauled him off.

"You pigs," he swore at them. "You'll ruin everything for her. And everyone else. You virgins, you make me sick."

Nakabe crawled away like a dog, though his eyes were still on Chieko's open legs and the red slash that bisected the smooth black triangle of hairs.

"Let me show you how." Jim's voice was soft and he reached for the buttons on his shirt.

She watched him strip, her eyes wide. Jim's body was well muscled, with only the hint of a belly, and without the bandy legs she had seen on Japanese men. From the juncture of his thighs projected something she had always wanted to see, and no less, to feel. His manhood greeted her with bows as he came towards her, then knelt between her legs. He separated her knees slowly, then bent forward and ran his tongue over her inner lips. Her hips bucked and she cried out in surprise. It was like the best of her dreams. Jim rose over her like a wave. She was moist, ready for him, her thighs glowing with inner heat.

The tip of his cock teased the entrance to her hole. She was so wet, her hairs matted with the juices of his tongue and her cunt, that he could not tell when he started piercing her body. She moaned gratefully as the engorged member penetrated her orifice. It was so much nicer than the objects she had used before, nicer even than her own fingers. Chieko urgently pushed a hand between their bodies to feel the penetration. Jim raised his body to accommodate her without releasing his intense pressure on her hips. She felt the long shaft and the folding of her inner lips over it. It was going in so deep, but there was still more to come. She touched the crisp hairs at the base, and then very delicately felt the swollen scrotum and the two soft eggs inside. He smiled at her and she returned his smile tentatively.

His belly touched hers and their hairs entwined. Jim lowered his lips slowly to hers. His tongue explored her warm mouth and she responded with movements of her own. He moved inside her, now that her inner channel was stretched and ready to accept him. She gasped at his weight but accepted it as part of the pleasure. Her fingers on his back urged him on.

Jim started shafting her rapidly, his cock shuttling in and out of the bowl of her thighs. She sighed contentedly, then gasped as an orgasm built up inside her. For a moment she was ashamed of the other men looking on, then she let herself go and her hips jerked with rapid tremors.

Ito and Nakabe were crouched on the mat staring, their eyes wide with anticipation. Jim motioned to Nakabe. He took Nakabe's hands and put them on the girl's soft, inviting breasts. Nakabe squeezed the flattened mounds greedily. His thumbs twiddled her nipples and he wondered at the warm rubberiness of her flesh, something he had never touched before.

Ito was panting heavily and looking at Jim in earnest supplication. Jim took the thin man's hand and guided it between his and Chieko's legs to her sopping cunt. Ito followed the unspoken instructions and stroked the overheated lips, coming into contact with Jim's long shaft as it moved lazily into the girl. Jim raised his torso high, supporting himself on one hand, and found the girl's clitoris with the other. He pinched and rubbed the vulnerable bit of flesh, carefully hiding and uncovering it with the upper part of her lips.

Chieko felt five male hands on her. She wanted to call out loudly in her pleasure, but contented herself with raising her face to Jim and then to Nakabe for a kiss, her tongue licking at their lips. Jim's movements quickened as he began to reach a climax. Ito could feel the swelling of his balls, and Chieko managed to snake a hand between their bodies again. She grunted and raised her hips in an urgent rhythm as she felt the male hands feeling her, then finally indentified the contraction of Jim's balls for what it was.

They burst into orgasm together. Chieko's innards were flooded with sperm. The spurt of male juices swept her into her own orgasm so powerfully she almost fainted. Jim impaled her with his cock, as if to drill through her. Ito found Jim's organ jerking in his hand, and then his fingers were covered with the overflow of sticky white fluid. He jerked his fingers back, then examined the fluid with curiosity. It was no different from the result of his own masturbation. Nakabe felt the girl's body twist. Her nipples had hardened to sharp points, and as she opened her eyes and her movements slowed, the little buds collapsed in his fingers as if exhausted.

Jim lay on the girl allowing his cock to soak in their mutual juices. Her hand roved over his back. At last, when the movements of her hips indicated she was attempting to raise him again, he slipped regretfully from her full cunt. Nakabe took his place, kneeling between her open thighs and arms. Jim leaned back and sipped at some whisky while Nakabe and the girl set to work. Ito squeezed the girl's breasts, waiting for his own turn.

"It was nicest with you," she said later, softly as she stacked the dishes. "I would like to come again."

He nodded. There were many things to be done with a willing girl, things he did not necessarily feel he should share with two novices such as Ito and Nakabe.

"Of course. Come whenever you please. Even without Nakabe-san."

"I will not see him again . . ."

"Of course you will. He is a good man. And from a rich family. Perhaps he will make you a good husband . . ."

She turned away to go. The thought had not occurred to her before. Jim grimaced at her back. The last thing he wanted was to have her hanging about permanently. Nakabe would take good care of her. Watching the girl, Jim missed the sharp look on Ito's face, which was briefly less epicine than it appeared when he'd been drunk.

CHAPTER 4:
Old Friends Remembered

For all its modern atmosphere Andy did not care for Shinjuku-West. The tall ultra-modern buildings were well spaced, the malls between them broad. Their foundations, beyond the park to the west, were tangled in the small two-story wooden houses of an urban neighborhood that. exemplified the contrast of modern Japan.

It had taken him several weeks and a few telexes to trace the WorldView Foundation, which had paid for his tuition and was now paying for his apartment, and the Nisei Education fund which had done the same for Jim. The tracks had led through New York and Switzerland, to Hong Kong, and finally to the Three Best Corporation, whose offices were supposedly in the Mitsui Building, Shinjuku.

Only they were not. There was a ShoKuBai Company on the premises, and they refused to supply him with any information. Two things were puzzling. Why wasn't the track covered more carefully? After all, as an aspiring financier, Andy knew how easy it would have been to hide the trail of any money fund. And, if it wasn't hidden, why the closed door at ShoKuBai? He considered what the name meant: plum, bamboo, and pine—the three best.

He stood for a long time in the glassed lobby of the building. Out of the corner of his eye he recognized the secretary he had spoken to, going out to lunch. He followed her. She was a large girl for a Japanese, with sturdy, shapely legs that showed through the slit in her calf-length skirt. She had been rather curt with him, and wore a continuous look of disapproval for the world.

She made her way through the jumble of shops near the Keio Department store, and crossed the tracks through the underground tunnel. A man in a poorly made business suit watched Andy pass, and followed him casually, in the direction of Hanazono-shrine. When the *gaijin* stopped at the entrance to Isetan, he stopped as well, and looked at one of the displays.

Andy had seen the girl disappear into the crowd in Isetan. He had moved quickly, but by the time he made it to the entrance, she was gone. He searched the ground floor carefully, through the throngs of women. No luck. Depressed by his double failure, he stood at the main entrance, debating whether to return home to work or to clear the air with a visit to a bookshop. His attention was drawn to a group of women walking past. There were five, only two of them Japanese. The other three, dressed in kerchiefs, long pajama-like shirts, and tight pantaloons were probably Pakistani's, judging by their pale color. He smiled at their backs, lost in memory as he looked at one of them whose full buttocks swayed before him. She was dressed in a green patterned suit which reminded him of Amina. The thought of her moved him to act, and he followed, overtaking the small group just as they turned into the store itself. He turned back to look at their faces, but his steps faltered. The one in green he had been admiring in memory of Amina, was Amina herself. Their eyes locked for a second, saw the shock of recognition on her fine features.

Hypnotized, he followed the small group as they chatted their way through the department store's displays. Amina looked ostentatiously at her watch, then said something to her companions in Urdu. She left them fingering some scarves, and swayed on her high-heeled slippers to the bank of red public telephones by the escalator.

"I didn't know you were in Tokyo," she murmured as she fumbled in her purse.

Andy picked up the handset and said his address and telephone number into it. She wrote it with a gold pencil in a small gilt-edged notebook, without looking at him. She looked prosperous. He assumed she'd made the successful marriage her father had hoped for.

"Tomorrow morning, I'm free. I'll call."

He opened the door and let her in silently. She stepped out of her slippers and into his waiting arms. Her tongue explored his mouth and she moaned happily at their meeting.

Alone in the apartment, they sat side by side on his wide bed. She diddled his cock through his robe as he slipped her shirt off her head and then undid her pants.

"I'm married now," she said. Her eyes were bright and she licked her red-painted lips. He knew fully what she meant by those simple words.

Three years before, Andy had been watching Amina, the Pakistani girl in his Japanese class, for some weeks. She seemed so aloof in her enveloping uniform of shapeless long shirt and pantaloons. A scarf hid the glory of her black hair. There was something inviting about the way she wore the clothes, as if they were there to be taken off, there to expose rather than hide. She had a warm complexion and regular features. When she bent down over her desk he could see the fabric stretch tight over a smooth round bottom that reminded him of a ripe peach. Her shirt was always closed at the neck. Andy was also aware that she never wore a bra. Her full breasts moved enticingly under the fabric, the nipples expanding and collapsing with changes to her mood. He had never expected to see her framed in the door of his student apartment.

"May I come in?" she said in her Indian-accented English.

"Of course." He led her into the tiny *yojohan* apartment he was living in at the time and offered tea.

She drank daintily, and nibbled at the cake on her plate, silent the whole while. Her black eyes roved over the apartment noting the details of the tiny four *tatami*-matted room.

"You have been watching me," she said eventually.

He nodded, forcing a confident smile, unaccountably nervous.

"I like that." Her eyes shone like black stars enhanced by the black kohl heavily applied to her long lashes. "I have never tasted a European. But I am due to get married, as soon as my father can find me a husband. My husband must take my virginity on my wedding night or I will be very ashamed. Or worse." He studied her face as she talked. He had never heard a girl talk so frankly before.

"Still, I like you. I think you like me." She stood up and slipped open the drawstring of her trousers. The pantaloons fell and pooled at her feet. Her belly was a beautiful curve shading down into the v of an almost hairless mound. Her large dark eyes were luminous in the pale oval of her face. She shuffled around and craned her neck back to look at him over her shoulder. She raised the tails of her long shirt.

Andy gazed for a long moment at her exposed buttocks. They were fully rounded, golden in color like a peach. She looked at him over her shoulder, enjoying his scrutiny.

"Remember," Amina whispered, "I must still be a virgin. Fuck my asshole. Bugger me. Get your cock into my ass. I love it." She bent forward prosaically, resting her head on his desk. Her long-fingered hands spread her full ass exploring the length of the crack. Her cunt-lips were prominent and plump. A small mossy growth shadowed the front. Above he could see, fully exposed to his gaze, the bud of her anus.

She grinned at him over her shoulder, then whispered commandingly "Come on my hero, come on you cock. Bugger me. Shoot it up my entrails. Fuck my ass, don't stop. You can have my mouth afterwards, but first I want to come from your cock in my anus. Come on!!!"

Andy lurched forward and aimed his cock mercilessly at the entrance while her hand shadowed the more precious entry to her vagina. He rammed forward and felt his cock sink into her slick internal recesses with an ease he had never experienced before. She hunched herself back at him impaling herself as he groped for her full breasts. He stood that way for a long moment savoring the feeling, and then she began constricting her sphincter around his shaft.

Andy moaned deliriously at the constriction, clutched at her generous hips below the shirt, and started a forceful motion which brought sounds of delight from her and a beatific smile. Her hole gripped him like a vice, though she had taken care to lubricate it generously with an unguent that smelled of roses. He watched the reddened staff disappear in the valley between the moons of her buttocks. The anal muscles clung to it, sucking as it re-emerged. He thrust forward again, into her. She murmured endearments in Japanese, English and Urdu. This time as he pulled out she fought his cock every inch of the way, squeezing her rear muscles for all she was worth. His withdrawal was painful, and he paid for it. She resisted his push with her anal muscles while at the same time forcing her full buttocks back at him.

They groaned together and Andy started forcing himself, shuttling his long cock in and out. She responded with glee, encouraging him with hungry cries, squeezing his hands into her full breasts. His explosion as he came lifted her off her feet. She forced her buttocks onto him one final time and contracted the muscles hard, squeezing his jet into her with a force that triggered her own orgasm. His mouth sought hers and he forced his tongue roughly between her teeth. They collasped together onto the desk. He lay on her breathing hard, his eyes closed. He was conscious of her long fingers exploring his stones in their hairy bag; the only part of his genitals that protruded from her behind. She touched herself dreamily, rubbing their essences together into her ass until the muscular rhythm drove his shrinking cock out of her.

"I must go, my knight. I have been here long enough, and I do not wish others to speak ill of me." He stood back and she cleaned his cock off with tissue paper she took from her purse.

"You can have me whenever you want," she said as he straightened the last of her clothing. "You are the best I have had. I am yours, my knight. All but my virginity which must remain for my husband-to-be. I am your bitch, you understand? I will do anything for you . . ."

"Except this," Andy said, clutching her crotch.

"Except that," she said calmly. "I cannot marry you. I must marry whomever my father decrees. But I can have fun. Does this disturb you? Would you like to beat me for your loss? Here—my buttocks, my breasts, my feet, even my face. They are yours. I will find pleasure in whatever you do to me for your own delight."

He looked at her for a moment, knowing he could believe every word. His hands shot forward and slapped her breasts. Their softness jiggled under his hand. They did not look as

they had ever been confined by a bra. She smiled at him. He
spun her around, again fully aroused. Her pantaloons were
down by her ankles in a second. His hard prick nuzzled the
tight hole of her rear for only a moment, and he was past the
ring of muscle. He jerked fiercely, once, twice, then spewed
himself into her channel.

He pulled out and pulled up her pants, then spun her
around again.

"Like that?"

"Yes," she said. "I shall carry your seed within me the
rest of this day."

He forced her to her knees. "Clean me!" Obediently she
sucked the slime from his cock and cleaned its softening
length. He raised her to her feet more gently.

"You'll come again?"

"Of course." Her large eyes were luminous. "As often as
I can, so long as I am near you. But only for a short while
each time," she said, knotting the drawstring of her pantaloons. "I must protect my reputation."

In the months that followed Amina had taught him much
about pleasing himself with her. Andy's lovemaking had been
straightforward and uninspired. Innate shyness kept him from
exercising his imagination with the women he had slept with
before. Amina changed all that, and he regretted her return to
her home immensely.

Now she was here and his again, sprawled in languid
curves on his bed. She had put on some weight. Her mound
was completely shaven, but she exhibited the same soft lush-
ness she had displayed before. She held the lips of her cunt
open with one hand, and gently stroked the depths with the
other.

"This is now permitted to you, my knight."

Andy wet his lips and advanced on the bed.

"One moment," she whispered, holding up the hand that had held the lips open. Don't you wish to examine your prize first?"

He knelt before the bed and inspected her offering. The outer lips were full and plump. The inner lips protruded a little. She peered over her mounded breasts, watching him as she spread the lips, exposing the bright red channel between them. Her fingers stroked the tiny clitoris, and one dipped into the hole. He bent forward and kissed her lightly, his tongue dipping into her.

"Oh no, my knight," she murmured. "You must not abase yourself so. *I* must do that for you . . ."

"Shut up," he said and slapped the inside of each thigh. "I will do what I want with you."

She squeaked and subsided, and he continued his exploration. He felt the insides of her lips, rubbing them between his fingers, and examined her as far in as he could see, spreading the moist convoluted tube with his fingers. It was a long time since he had had the opportunity to do this. He began testing the reactions of her cunt to various possibilities. He noted the quivering of her thighs and her muttered endearments as he touched her clitoris, labiae, and inner channel, and stroked the opening to her urethra. Her quivers grew as he proceeded. He continued touching her lightly, with his fingers and occasional laps of his tongue. The touching quickened and she stiffened. Her belly jerked at his fingers and he watched as her channel moistened with her own fluid. She moaned enticingly in her own language.

She recovered and raised her head to watch his erection as he stood between her spread legs.

"Please wait, my knight. I can be a virgin for you too."

Puzzled, he followed her lead. From her bag she extracted a condom.

He grinned. "I don't really need that, particularly not for *you!*" he said.

"Look at it again," she commanded handing him the rubber tube. It was studded with long stiff barbs and knobs

"It will hurt you like hell," Andy exclaimed in surprise.

"It will indeed," she nodded. "It might even make me bleed a little. It will be painful, and I will be like a virgin for you. My reactions will give you pleasure, as your triumph will give me. Wear it."

Andy slipped the tickler on and she gently manipulated and sucked his prick until it expanded and filled the tube tightly. Then she lay back, spreading her legs and raising her behind from the bed. Andy threw himself on her.

He diddled the entrance of her lush warmth for a moment. She exuded moisture. An arm covered her eyes as with the other hand she clutched at the sheet with anticipation. He thrust home and she shrieked in earnest as the spines ripped at the sides of her vagina. He pushed again and again as her shrieks filled his ears and her face contorted under him, until he was lodged fully in her body. For a moment he rested on her and she panted beneath him. He withdrew slightly and she moaned with pain, though her hands were now clutching at his straining buttocks. He pushed forward and heard her whimper. Almost withdrawing, he plunged in again to meet a shudder of pain and pleasure. She was now better lubricated and he could slide in and out with greater ease. As he moved her cries became softer, were replaced with the sound of pleasure. Her belly was soon covered with a sheen of perspiration, and she turned her eyes to his, murmuring comforting words mixed with descriptions of the power of his cock.

At last he trembled over her for a moment, then plunged down onto her, his full weight on the root of his cock, balanced on her clit. He wriggled like a fish caught on a hook, then drained himself into her in gushing throbs.

His cock shrank and he withdrew gently from her. She quivered and he slipped a hand under her shoulders as he lay down beside her, his other hand stroking her belly. Calmed, she turned to him.

"Don't you want to inspect the result of your prowess?" Amina demanded.

Obeying, he spread her suddenly reluctant legs and examined the ravages of his effort. There was a trace of blood mixed with the white glue that trickled from her. The lips were red and puffy, tender to his touch, but, he opened them to view her bruised interior. She trembled under his fingers, and he kissed the grazed clit, then withdrew his head as she pulled him up to her mouth.

Warm and comfortable, they stroked one another, waiting for lust to rise again. "What are you doing now? Why are you here?"

She shrugged and her pale brown breasts swayed. "I live in Islamabad, with my husband and two children. . . ."

"Two children?"

"Indeed," she chuckled. "Did you think I would be infertile? Mainly I am a housewife, thought I sometimes teach women about Japan."

"What a waste of an education. Surely you could have done better?"

"I have done very well," she insisted. "I come to Tokyo to shop several times a year, as well as to London or New York. I can afford it; my husband keeps me well."

"What does he do?"

"Let's not talk of him," she said shortly. "Let us talk of you."

He told her of his unremarkable career to date, then mentioned his new-found brother.

"Ah, you see," she said. "That comes of not being careful." She held up her breasts and squeezed them. "We know that women are lustful, but if one is careful to use one's ass and tits, then what is the harm? And my husband is very satisfied." She rose to go.

CHAPTER 5:
Pleasure Bent

Adjusting the waistband of her pantyhose through her plain grey skirt, Teruko Uabashi decided for the hundredth time that she was an unlucky woman. Her figure was ungainly, her abilities poor, and her luck such that at times she despaired of living. She was even terrible about her pleasures, as witness the previous day.

It was not that she was particularly lustful. Matsuoka-san, the new office clerk had been so out of place that she had merely taken pity on him. The group of office mates had gone out for lunch, and over a beer—one too many—Matsuoka described his lonely bachelor's life. This was his third job; he had left the others apparently, because, loneliness had become too much for him. He described how he would sit in front of the television in his small apartment, go for walks, and work, the sum of his life. So he had moved on, desperate, hoping for some solace.

Teruko found it surprising. He was a youngish man, pleasant, with nice hands, and painfully shy, which she rather liked. She had gone shopping Sunday in the downtown mall under Yokohama train station and met him purely by chance.

45

His greeting had been shy as usual, but there was something wistful about his expression. She was about to have a snack, and invited him to join her. He had acquiesced gratefully. Walking past the restaurants with their plastic food displays she had discovered that as a native of Chugoku province he had never eaten *tonkatsu,* the Yokohama specialty of deep-fried pork fillet.

After eating she had intended to continue her shopping. But she had invited him to come with her, and although hesitantly, he agreed. One thing led to another, and before long they were pouring a white Australian wine he had bought into two tumblers in her two-room apartment.

"This is a nice place," he said, looking around. She was an indifferent housekeeper, but enjoyed decorating her surroundings with flowers and colorful paintings.

"Oh no," she protested modestly, holding a hand over her mouth.

"Have some more wine?" He poured her a glass. She could see he was nervous. His hands were trembling. She rose to fetch some more *eda mame,* green soy beans boiled in salt water. As her sleeve brushed the glass, he grabbed for it. It slipped and rolled across the table. They grabbed at it together with cries of dismay. Wine soaked them.

"I'm so sorry, so terribly sorry," they said at the same time, standing up together. She surveyed his wet trousers. "You must change . . ."

Matsuoka looked at her. "You too," he pointed out.

She left him with a *yukata* robe that her husband had left behind after the divorce, slid the door closed between the rooms and took off her wet skirt. Her eye caught the image in the mirror. Through the frosted glass that glazed the modern-style *shoji* sliding door behind her that separated the rooms, she could see his outline as he dropped his pants and jacket, reaching for the *yukata* on the tatami beside him.

On impulse, wearing no expression, and no skirt, she opened the sliding door.

"Matsuoka-san, may I help you?"

He turned, startled, and dropped the *yukata*. "No, no . . ." he said, blushing. His protests died in his throat as he saw she was skirtless. She slid forward and knelt at his feet. He had nice legs, she noted.

She picked up the *yukata*, saying "You will be most uncomfortable in your shirt. Please, let me . . ." Before he could react, she had risen to her feet, unbuttoning his shirt as she stood. There was a perceptible bulge in his shorts. His eyes glazed as he smelled the powder on her face. She slipped the shirt from his shoulders, then removed his undershirt. Pressing herself against him, she dropped her clothes and pulled him down to the floor beside her.

She was not surprised by his fumbling lovemaking. The only man she had known was her husband. Once or twice a month he would turn her on her back in the dark of the night, and mount her. She enjoyed the feel of his cock and his hands and lips, and though her husband was not rough, she often wished he were more demanding. She would readily forgive his violence, she often thought, if it had carried over into his lovemaking. But she had always been too shy, too afraid of being forward. When he had left her, she was too embarrassed to masturbate or take a lover, and her urges had grown. Even her former husband's violence titillted her in her dreams, associated as it was with the only sexual pleasure she had known.

Matsuoka launched himself onto her desperately as she spread her legs in welcome. The warm fleshy rod jammed against her crotch, sometimes missing entirely in his excitement, sometimes hitting the entrance or rubbing against the damp hairs, but never penetrating. She grasped him with a firm hand and guided him in. His eyes widened and he uttered strangled cries as the knob on his prick felt the soft warmth. He lurched forward, burying his cock in her to its roots. He lay dazed for a long moment. Then, trying to shield the motion by sucking hungrily on her prominent nipples, he felt the root of his cock and the lips of her cunt. He was well inside her and he smiled his satisfaction: At last.

He began to oscillate rapidly with his bottom. There was a fathomless urge, quite different from when he masturbated, to fountain the liquid that boiled in his balls. As he jogged in and out, she urged him on with movements of her pelvis. She met each thrust with raised hips, and her fingers clawed at his back while she licked his face and lips. In the wildness of his movements he found suddenly that his cock was in the air. Desperately he searched again for the heavenly opening, but found only her smooth belly. She reached down again to find and help him, but suddenly he was overcome. His cock pumped milky fluid over the dome of her stomach, sticking him to her as it ran over their skin. He tried to stop himself, but it was hopeless.

Sobbing drily he clung to her, his fingers digging into her soft behind. She moved her hips to encourage him, knowing that within a few minutes she would be able to bring him to the ready again. He misinterpreted the movement, and thought she was pushing him off. He rose to his knees, without looking at her. He smelled the sharp odor of his own fluids. She looked at him in bewilderment. She raised a spunk-stained hand to stop him from moving away and he misunderstood that, too as an admonishment. He backed away in shame, as if to apologize for soiling her fingers and belly.

As he backed out the door with his tie and jacket loose, he read her accusing face. He wished he could stay. He wished that shame of his grossness and inability to perform, did not color his expression. He looked at her one last time, for the sight of her figure. Her smooth rounded belly shiny with his emission and the dark triangle of her hair stayed in his mind as he made his way home.

Teruko had watched in surprise as he had dressed. It was incomprehensible that he would abandon her like that. There must have been something that turned him off, her forwardness, some smell, touch or taste he did not care for. She wished he had stayed, and given her a chance to apologize. Sadly, she dressed.

She was daydreaming about Matsuoka, who had not come in to the office that morning, when a human sound interrupted the mechanical whir of the air conditioner.

"Excuse me, ah . . ." Jim saw her nameplate, guessed at the Chinese characters "Ah . . . Uabashi-san. My name is Suzuki Jinsuke. I am preparing a report on small computers in financial firms. Perhaps you can help me?" He handed her his card.

She was, Jim decided, rather attractive, with a smooth plump face, with just a dusting of freckles, and a small, imperfectly made up mouth. There were circles under her eyes; if not for the expression of disdain she wore, he would have called her beautiful. He could see the tops of a plump pair of breasts under her carelessly done blouse.

By lunchtime she had discovered that he knew computers, offices, and a surprising lot about herself. Much of her petulant mood had vanished. They ate lunch at a place he knew in Kabukicho, the entertainment area east of the tracks. The tiny restaurant—traditional and very expensive—was one she would never have been able to try on her own. The *bento* lunch was served, each morsel of food nestling gorgeously in its own compartment in the lacquered tray placed before them. She was afraid to say she could not afford such a meal, and was grateful when, without asking or saying a word, he paid for them.

Teruko watched Jim covertly throughout the meal. He was

smooth muscled and moved with an easy confidence. He smiled directly into her eyes and was considerate of her, lighting the sole cigarette she timidly allowed herself. Some of the hurt of her incapacity with Matsuoka ebbed away. The memory of the encounter still brought shame to her face and she had not dared see him alone since. Matsuoka himself had kept a stiff face in her presence and did not speak to her. Suzuki-san, on the other hand, did not seem to mind her crude unfamiliarity with the restaurant or the food she had heard about but could never afford to taste before. He was not even defensive about his own disability: His mixed parentage, to which he admitted freely and cheerfully, volunteering the information that he did not know which of his parents was Japanese and whether they had been married or not.

They walked out of the tiny place and Suzuki-san took her arm in a courtesy that she had seen, but was otherwise also unfamiliar with. They talked gaily as they walked through the narrow alleys, decorated by the fronts of eating and drinking places, theaters and strip shows. She giggled shyly as he pointed out the displays of a strip joint, and she called his attention to the giant crab whose claws waved outside an establishment that catered to admirers of the crustacean.

He looked into her eyes and smiled. She smiled back, and her eyes focused on a sign behind his shoulder, of one of the many love hotels in *Kabukicho*. The rooms were rented by the hour for couples whose homes and apartments were too small to indulge themselves in. For a second she wondered what it would be like with Suzuki-san. She was very conscious of his hand on her elbow, and slowly moved towards him, her mouth slightly open, her eyes staring at the sign.

Jim turned his head slightly and saw the sign out of the corner of his eye. His hold tightened slightly, and he guided her under the blue awning into the cool interior. They crossed a tiny stone bridge and he slid a ten-thousand yen bill through

the window, receiving a key in exchange. She walked down
the corridor by his side, dazed by her own audacity. They
stepped into the room and he turned to her at the foot of the
wide bed. Mirrors adorned the ceiling and walls, and the
blank eye of a VTR over the larger one of a TV set greeted
them.

Her knees trembled and she fell onto the coverlet.

Jim looked at her, her face hidden, legs askew, her dark
hair covering her head. She was sobbing or breathing hard, he
couldn't tell. He had no idea what her problem was, but
clearly unless he acted soon, he would get nothing from her.

He ran his palms up her legs without any response. Her
skirt came off quickly, then her pantyhose and panties. He
kissed her smooth buttocks once, then again. There was no
response beyond a tensing of the long muscles in her thighs.
He turned her over. She lay still, her eyes open and staring at
him blankly. Her jaw was tight. He kissed her lips and they
parted to allow his tongue access, but she was passive, afraid
a response would drive him away, like Matsuoka. He smiled
at her, but her face remained frozen. He hurriedly stripped
her upper garments off and she lay before him naked, as he
undressed rapidly in turn. Her full belly rose and fell with her
breathing. Her bush was full and fluffy, and he kissed it, then
tongued the tip of her slit. She clenched her thighs, as if
unfamiliar with the sensation. He raised his head, puzzled.
The tension was still there, stiffening her face.

Teruko stared at the ceiling. She saw herself ugly and
strained, staring back. The man's dark head had lingered over
her nipples as they stiffened pleasurably in response. Then
the dark head above the blue suit had withdrawn and the male
figure was foreshortened as he undressed. She could see in
the mirror, that he had no real desire for her. The dark head
descended again, this time to the juncture of her legs. She
cried out involuntarily and closed her thighs. She had heard

of such practices whispered in the girls' room in school, but this sensation was startling, something that was completely unnatural. He withdrew and she clenched her hands and her eyes, squeezing out tears. He stepped off the bed and walked to the bathroom. It was over, she thought now. The tears pooled in the corners of her eyes. Better to be dead than to be disappointed and to disappoint as she did. She heard him fumbling in the bathroom and began to rise, groping for her clothes.

Jim found the machines he had expected in a corner of the bathroom. He put in the coins and returned to the bed with the small bottle of lotion. She froze in the act of reaching for her clothes, her hair obscuring her face. Her body was twisted in a pleasing pose and he smiled, then knelt on the bed and reached for her. Passively she allowed him to push her flat. He laved her stomach with some of the lotion and began rubbing it in. The tension in her stomach muscles gradually subsided. His hands described wider circles and soon he was squeezing her breasts with one hand and the lips of her cunt near her clitoris with the other. She watched his actions in the overhead mirror for a long time, then surrendered to the sensation and closed her eyes.

He leaned forward and kissed her mouth. She tasted faintly of salt and of sweet things. His lips wandered over her torso, licking at the prominent nipples. With one hand he traced the harder muscles, softening them with his palm. With the other he teased the crease between the legs. A fire built up in the pit of her belly, something she had never felt before. She wished he were manipulating her sex with a firmer hand, with more power. Even a little bit of pain would please her. Her hips rose to meet his probing finger. Her lower torso started twisting, gradually matching the rhythm of his massaging hand. Her belly softened, and Jim rested his head on it for a moment. She smiled with the growing demands of her own body.

Jim placed his erect cock in her hand. She felt the long shaft, and the soft stones within their wrinkled bag. Then the power of the sensations he was rousing with his fingers and his lips took over. His tongue descended into her warm eager depths. She groaned and forced the probing tongue down into her, spreading her legs and raising her knees. Jim enjoyed the taste and wet of her, not minding the fact that in her excitement she ignored him almost completely. She thrashed about under him. Her hips arched as far as they could go and she felt an unstoppable wave of lust envelop her. She twitched wildly, her head flailing. Inadvertently his teeth closed on her clitoris as she forced his face down. The hard touch of the teeth and the nip of pain set Teruko's orgasm off. She squealed "Bite it, bite me, . . . o . . o . . . Suzuki-san, bite me please, please," as her juices coated his tongue and lips. Jim tried to pull back, surprised at her reaction and enjoying his power over her, but her body refused to subside. Waves of a pleasure she had glimpsed but never reached before washed over her. Teruko wanted it to go on forever. Gradually, though with many smaller peaks of sensation and delight, her orgasm faded.

Teruko came to herself and looked at the man beside her. She could barely remember his name. He was looking at his still-erect cock with an unfathomable expression on his face. Suddenly she realized what she had done. She had had her pleasure, but she had been unsuccessful once more, as with Matsuoka-san, in behaving as a proper woman. She saw that he would disdain anything she could offer now.

Teruko gave a strangled cry and threw herself off the bed. Locking herself in the bathroom, she dressed, trembling. She did not respond to his knocks or his calling.

Pleased with his ability at pleasing her, Jim had been

considering how to proceed. He had shaken his cock experimentally, wondering whether to wake her. Suddenly, she had leapt from the bed, grabbed her clothing, and locked herself in the bathroom. He had called her for a long time, growing angry. Unable to figure out what had caused the reversal in her behavior, he threw on his own clothes and left.

Walking with frustration through the narrow alleys of *Kabukicho,* Jim bumped into a passer-by. He mumbled an excuse, and only raised his head when he felt the blow against his shoulder. The man before him in a checked brown jacket raised his hand for a second blow. Reflexes took over. Jim flung his hand out and knocked the other man away, pushing straight out at the attacker's face. Before the man could recover, Jim was running down the alley in the direction he'd come from.

He doubled and twisted through the streets, keeping to the crowded ones, then boarded the green Yamanote train heading in the direction of Shibuya and home. Once he had regained his composure and assured himself that his attacker was nowhere around, he pondered the attack. The man was not drunk; Jim had no memory of the smell of liquor. But he had shouted something, something that Jim was not to do. The memory of Teruko and her nervousness seemed to make things clearer. Irate boyfriends or husbands were to be avoided whenever possible, but it was annoying that she had not warned him ahead of time.

Nearer home, Andy stepped diffidently into the housing agent's office.

"Ah, Middler-san," Ishida, the housing agent, had the grace to blush, which meant she knew what was going on. Or she thought he was here to renew their acquaintance.

"I was just walking by," he said. I was about to have some coffee . . . I wonder if you would like to join me?"

She thought about if for a moment. "Well, I had some shopping to do . . ."

"I would not like to bother you," he lowered his voice and looked at the ground. "But perhaps you would like to examine the equipment again . . . ?"

Ishida's neck colored slightly. She realized she had actually intended to come to his apartment for some time, but with circumstances as they were. . . . "I would like that," she said. There was a glint in her eye. "Perhaps. . . . perhaps you would come to my apartment for dinner? Tonight? I am a very poor cook of course . . ."

The apartment was a new Japanese style home of blonde wood and fresh green-yellow *tatami* mats. Ishida, Andy found, was a woman of many talents. A perfectly executed Ohara school flower arrangement sat before a scroll in the *tokonoma* alcove. There were prints on the wall. She seemed to like *hashira-e,* the long, narrow eighteenth-century prints that had just returned to style. There was a photograph of a younger Ishida with a man, perhaps a husband. Divorced? Widowed? Abandoned? Andy was reluctant to ask. She was dressed in a full kimono when she bowed him into the room. Andy was amazed she had managed to arrange all this in the two hours since they had parted. The meal was excellent, catered by *Fukiya,* a restaurant in Akasaka to which Andy would not have been allowed entry, even assuming he had the ready cash for it. Barbarians and children were not welcome at the high-wall Japanese restaurants.

She had served. Warm sake. Fresh *sashimi* with native lime and soy sauce. Steamed squash and pickles. Sweet carp. *Chawanmushi* custard. Between courses Andy gradually forgot about Jim's troubles, and his amusement at his partner's problems with the secretary's boyfriend. He expressed his admiration at Ishida's choice and insisted that she join him, which she did after much hesitation. He drained the tiny sake cup, then filled it again and passed it to her. She smiled and drank; he poured her another.

"How long have you worked for this agency?"

"Oh, I am part-owner. The other partner is Daisan Corporation. They own many properties in Japan." She smiled. "They are also your landlords, though under another name: Cloud Corporation. Taxes and organizational efficiency, you know."

"I'm interested," Andy said. "Part of my research is concerned with financing, and real estate companies in Japan are generally tied in with other interests."

"O yes, Daisan has many interests. For example, their president is a major art collector, and they own art galleries as well. He is a very retiring man, but a great financier. They are not actually a Tokyo corporation. I believe they are based in Nagoya, but I deal with their local offices here."

She cleared the dishes and returned to sit by the table, deftly peeling a soft ripe persimmon. She sat opposite him, on the other side of the low table, and Andy decided it was time to move the evening along. A slippery piece of the orange fruit fell to the *tatami* by his side. She hurriedly moved towards him and picked it up. She raised her head to meet his gaze. Another piece of persimmon was between his lips. He bent forward, hand at the nape of her neck where the crisp collar of her robe met an escaped curl of hair. The persimmon slice touched her lips. Reluctantly she opened them. As she started to bite, to divide the morsel in half, he forced it further in until the whole of it rested on her tongue. He explored her teeth gently with his tongue, then withdrew it slightly, the pressure of his lips on hers still firm. She chewed the slice slowly, enjoying the juicy, viscous feel of the sweet fruit. He licked her lips as she chewed and she savored the male flavor of his mouth as well. She swallowed; another slice was pressed to her lips. It entered deeply into her and this time his tongue explored her mouth, with the fruit before withdrawing. The slice was smaller and she swallowed it whole. His lips tasted the angle of her jaw and returned to her mouth. More fruit followed. She closed her eyes slowly as the slick sensation permeated her mouth. His lips never left hers, his tongue licking her teeth as she chewed and swallowed. Warmth grew in her loins and she rubbed her thighs together slowly. There was one last piece of fruit. He put it to his mouth and applied his lips to hers again. She felt the exquisite softness of the pulped fruit flowing along his tongue and into her mouth. Her eyes shut and the lower reaches of her belly flashed with a heat that peaked and retreated but did not go away. She sucked the pulp down.

Andy rose to his knees and Ishida bent forward. A warm slick morsel pressed between her lips. They parted and she sucked hungrily. The tip exuded a nectar similar to the persimmon's in taste and texture, but slightly salty. Her lips moved along the shaft as her tongue explored the flared head. Andy looked down and saw his erect penis disappear into her mouth. He could barely see her red lips extruding and retracting as she took her delight from this fruit. He pushed forward slightly and more of the shaft disappeared. She was on all fours now, her back straight and the elegant bow of her kimono sash obscuring the curve of her posterior.

Ishida sucked harder on Andy's protrusion, the volcano in her belly rising to a new eruption. She pulled, her cheeks hollowing. Andy groaned above her and his sperm rose in a thick rush, filling her mouth with the acrid flavor. The shaft forced itself to her throat and she swallowed smoothly, delighted as her own insides released their moisture, too.

Ishida pulled back and Andy sank to his knees. She slowly opened her eyes and looked at him, her dark almond-shaped eyes fathomless. He offered her a cup of sake. Wordlessly Ishida shook her head, turning sideways and bowing slightly.

Andy's arm went around her shoulder. He kissed the nape of
her neck and nibbled the expanse of shoulders not covered by
the gown. He slipped his hand down her back until he found
the *obi* bow. He fumbled slightly and she wondered whether
he was about to spoil their fun with ineptitude. To her
surprise, Ishida found that Andy knew his way around a
kimono. He loosened the end of the *obijime,* the silken
armor-cord that held the *obi* sash in place. His hands followed the stiff sash around to her front and undid the yellow
cord, then dipped into the wide sash. She supported her back
straight with her hands flat on the mat while he undid the
tie-dyed bustle. His hands moved smoothly back again and
gently, with no hurry, removed the intricate folds that made
up the knot of the *obi* at the small of her back. The stiff cloth,
patterned with silver and blue clouds, slithered to the mat.
Andy crouched behind her, his lips never ceasing their nibbling at her shoulders, at the nape of her neck, tugging
slightly at the long dark strands that were beginning to fall
from the pins on her hair.

He found the opening to the kimono. The raw silk under-
robe she wore under her kimono was open. Like the kimono,
it had been closed only by the *obi* sash. He raised his hands
and felt the length of her torso. The skin was smooth and
taut. Her breasts, hanging free, were hard with anticipation,
the nipples erect, full. Her ribs moved beneath his hands, her
heart pounding inside. Her belly, though full and softened
with age, now held a delicious tension. His fingers reached
the upper hairs between her legs and a small tremor started
and grew. It transmitted to her belly and rose to her arms, so
that by the time his fingers had reached her split, Ishida was
trembling like a leaf. His fingers dipped into the dark recess.
She shuddered and her mouth opened as her eyes shut. Andy
was aware of the wetness between her legs that caused the
lower hairs to stick to his palms, when the moisture flooded

with more liquid from her inner femininity. He stroked the slick hairs, closing the outer lips over her softening clitoris as the spasms subsided.

Andy rocked back and rose to his feet. His penis was fully erect again, held to his belly by his underpants. Ishida swivelled in place and rose as well. She closed her robe with her hand and hurriedly slid over the *tatami* to a corner of the small room. On a footed tray lay a bundle covered by a patterned cloth. She returned to Andy, standing by the table, with a male *yukata* robe of dark gray silk conical in both hands. She knelt and lay down the robe, then rose again to remove his jacket and undo his tie and shirt buttons. She slipped the garments off his shoulders and her long-nailed hands stroked his skin, lingering over his chest. Unable to contain herself, she leaned to him and hurriedly licked each male nipple in turn. The *yukata* went over Andy's shoulders and he put his arms into the loose sleeves. She knelt before him and undid his pants. They fell to the floor and his cock sprang from its thicket of dark brown hairs.

Slowly, she began licking her way up his legs. She reached his thighs and her tongue drew circles below his hanging sack. She pressed herself against his shins and knees, and he could feel the smooth warmth of her breasts. Ishida lapped the length of his maleness, gently sucking for a second at the tip, and rose higher. Inside the tent of their kimono, her naked body aligned with his. She sucked and kissed his nipples thoroughly, then stood to her full height and kissed the length of his collarbone to his jaw. Andy's hands roved inside her kimono, enjoying the full sensation of her body. Finally he clutched her full buttocks. She let out a gasp as his fingers dug into the softness. Her weight increased the discomfort as he raised her high up his belly. She assisted him with her heels, the white split-toed *tabi* socks digging into his calves.

The tip of Andy's cock nudged the wet entrance to her channel. Andy held her there for a moment, and she obligingly rubbed herself around the tip, her face buried in his shoulder. He lowered her gratefully onto his erection as he sank to the floor. Encased in the silken cocoon of their kimono, he moved his hips with intricacies that fanned their fires to a roaring blaze.

CHAPTER 6:
Japanese Doll

Jim's gloom at his failure in Shinjuku had worn off by the following morning, and they had a council of war. Andy's success with the land agent, Mrs. Ishida, had opened new possibilities. The apartment building owners would have to be investigated. Andy would visit their offices to see what there was in the way of information, while Jim would start over. Perhaps the hint they had gotten from Michiko Teraoka, the policewoman, offered an approach. She would probably be able to help Jim get the address of his putative "uncle"; the man so much like him who lived in Kita Ward. It was a slim lead, but they had precious little else.

Andy stepped into the bright office and looked around. He hoped his credentials were good enough. Many Japanese companies were shy about giving any sort of information to outsiders, particularly foreign ones.

"May I help you please?"

One look at the secretary changed his mind, as a different plan of action suggested itself. Slim and small, curly brown hair danced at her shoulders. More important, the smile she gave him had something suggestive in it. Andy introduced himself and explained his need, smiling boyishly as he did so.

". . . so you see, it is not easy doing research in Japan. I am a student, but everyone suspects me of trying to learn some deep dark secrets."

"Oh no, Middler-san. No one suspects you. Japanese all like foreigners, very much."

"Do you?" he asked bluntly. He had been talking in her office for all of fifteen minutes. Her boss, it turned out, would be out for the day.

She blushed slightly at the directness of his question and said briskly, "Yes, of course."

"Why then, let's have lunch together."

"But Middler-san, I hardly know you . . ." She pronounced his name "Midlaa" and the sound sent a peculiar warmth through him.

"Quite right," he said, standing. Then he bowed dramatically. "Middler, Andrew, at your service Madam."

She giggled. "Koihara Natsumi," and bowed at her desk.

"Miss Koihara, might I have the pleasure of your company for lunch? And dinner?"

She smiled brightly and said, "Of course, Midlaa-san."

"And you must call me Andy," he added. "Later then."

They ate *sushi* at the counter of a shop near the Ginza, then homemade ice-cream in Roppongi. She was a pleasant companion, Andy found as the evening wore on. Later, over drinks he suggested stopping at his apartment. She clung to his arm, her lithe body warm against his. Natsumi's eyes were filled with fun, and within them Andy felt he detected an impassioned glitter, something to examine leisurely, as they stepped up into the apartment.

The wine was as red as her lips, he thought, turning the lights low. She drank daintily, holding the long stemmed glass with both hands. Under her lashes she examined the apartment discreetly and decided she liked what she saw.

"Do you dance?" Andy asked as he turned on the stereo.

"Yes, Mr. Andy, I love it," Natsumi answered in a babydoll voice. He had been trying to break her of the habit of calling him by title the whole evening. Nonetheless, she continued. Andy wondered whether it was habit or intentional. The slow, dreamy music filled the room. She melted into his arms. The *tatami* shifted under the weight as they swayed in place. Her body had a peculiar contradictory feel to it; slim and full at once. She pressed into him with her full length, her hair just brushing his nostrils, her thighs contoured to his.

He began to respond. Imprisoned by her thighs against his tight pants, his growing member felt pain as it swelled for freedom. Experimentally, he rubbed his hips against her. She clung even tighter. His left hand disengaged from hers and he pulled her waist into him with both hands. She edged still closer, swaying to the music.

He slid his hands up and down her form. Her buttocks, though not full, were pleasantly rounded and her back was firm. Her black skirt was held by a zipper in the rear. He undid the hooks and slid the zipper head down.

"No, Mr. Andy, no please, you must not." The babydoll voice was tantalizing him again. She moaned against his chest but made no effort to get out of his arms. The skirt, aided by his hands, slipped easily over her hips and fell to the ground. Underneath she wore a sheer slip whose upper reaches hid beneath her black blouse. He felt her behind, patting and stroking the fabric over it. His erection pushed into her stomach and she rubbed herself against him.

"Please, I should go." Natsumi tried to step back. He held on to her, his lips at her neck.

"I must be home. I must get a taxi." But her hand stroked his arm.

"Not yet!" he said, panting.

"Yes, now." She kissed him. Her tongue dipped into his mouth and she sucked at him hungrily. "Goodbye," she said.

This time, as she had intended, his face suffused with anger. She resisted as he tried to lower her to the tatami. He let go and demanded "What the hell do you want?"

She moved back to him. "Please, Mr. Andy. Let us dance."

He acquiesced. She stuck to him again, and he felt the bowls of her thighs and belly supporting his renewed erection. But again she resisted when he tried to pull her to the floor. Andy would not have any more of it. He tripped her and they fell to the tatami mats. He sprawled on her and kissed her passionately, his tongue active and searching. His hands slid up her legs, his rough palm buzzing over the nylon. She attacked him with the palms of her hands, muttering unintelligible protests as she tried to push him off.

Exasperated, Andy's eyes lit on the scarf she had worn. He rolled her over quickly, grabbed the scarf, and in a few quick motions wrapped it around her wrists.

The scarf tight, he knelt back panting. She looked up at him, her eyes narrowed. He swallowed hard, then came forward and kissed her savagely. Her lips were as pliant and eager as they had been at first. He began unbuttoning her blouse.

"Please, Andy, what are you doing?"

He snorted. "Unbuttoning your blouse . . ."

"No please, you must not. I do not like that . . ."

He kissed her again, and she responded as before. The blouse came off her shoulders and gathered at her wrists. He slid the straps of her slip off her shoulders. She wore no bra underneath; kneeling by her side, he looked at her breasts. The dark brown nipples were tumescent. Thick as his little finger they overshadowed her small, rather flat breasts. Andy leaned forward again quickly and kissed her; her tongue licked out to meet his own. But when his hands took her nipples she squirmed and tried to push him away with her shoulders.

He drew back, then deliberately lowered his head to one nipple. "No, please Andy-san. You must not do this. I am ashamed. Please you must stop."

Ignoring her, he sucked in the entire length of the rubbery tip, then sucked on the soft breast as if to swallow it whole. She writhed beneath him, mewling with displeasure or delight: he could not tell. He moved his attention to the other breast, while he pinched and diddled the one made wet with his saliva. Her movements quickened and he saw out of the corner of his eye that her slip had ridden up her nylon covered thigh.

He pulled back.

"Andy-san, surely you do not do this with every girl who dances with you? You must let me go. I am very embarrassed like this. It is not nice."

He grinned at her. "I understand," he said. "It is nice and not nice." He gazed at her form for a moment as she tried to hide her face. Then kissing her neck gently, he slid his hands up her legs. Her thighs were fleshy but firm, and the feel of nylon was somewhat unpleasant. She muttered more, protesting. With one hand he pulled her to him, raising her buttocks off the floor. With his other hand he slid the hem of the undergarment to her hips. He licked his lips. She caught his gaze, focused on the veiled juncture of her legs, and turned her face away.

"I am ashamed," she said.

He put her roughly onto her side and she lay passively. He licked the side of her breast, then trailed his tongue down the curve of her body to the elastic of her pantyhose. He paused for a moment to stroke her plump behind, then hooked his fingers under the elastic. With one movement he pulled the hose and lacy white panties off her hips and down to her knees.

"No, no please," she whispered. Her lips were barely moving and her eyes were closed. "Please do not look."

He spread her legs and eased himself out of his pants, then took off his shirt. She panted below him, her golden skin marred faintly by the dimple of an appendix scar. The dark fur between her legs was smooth and thick, ending about an inch below her thin outer lips. He doubled himself over, and for one long delicious moment sucked at the slim lips. The outer labiae were dry, but once his tongue had penetrated to the inner recesses, he was conscious of an overwhelming moisture that came over his tongue.

He guided his erection forward to the entrance. She was wider than he had expected, and her moisture aided in the penetration. She moaned and opened her eyes slightly as his shaft filled her. He lay still for a second. She looked at his face through half-closed eyelids, waiting.

Andy pumped into Natsumi once, then again. She raised her hips to meet his and he was conscious that she was kicking off the constricting pantyhose.

"I'm going to punish you," he said.

"Yes Andy-san," she said dreamily.

"I'm going to punish you for putting me off this way." He pumped at her again, and she responded as before. Suddenly he pulled out of her. She started to protest, then reconsidered. "Please, you must stop," she said again.

He slid his hands over her body as he gradually brought her to a sitting position, then to *seiza;* the formal position on one's knees. He kissed her mouth and she responded deeply, drawing his tongue into her mouth, then licking at his teeth. His hand stroked her hair, then her jaw. Then he rose until his cock was pointed directly at her face, which he still held in his hands.

She had time to note how pink it was before he shoved it to her lips. Her mouth opened, and he slid himself slowly inside. She sucked deeply, hollowing her mouth and relaxing her throat to take his full length.

Andy felt the heat of her mouth, like a soft furnace that urged him deeper. He allowed her to suck him with her tongue, lips, and throat at once. He moved only slightly from side to side, testing her willingness. Before he burst, he pulled out and let the rigid cock rest against her cheek, stroking it with a trail of her saliva that marred her perfect makeup.

He lowered her onto her side again. She protested slightly as he took both of her tiny breasts and fucked them. He was much less gentle now, as the small soft mounds yielded to his penis.

They were both breathing heavily. Again he pulled away as the throbbing in the shaft warned him of his coming climax. He rubbed the cock over her belly now, the dimple of her navel and the scar. She protested softly.

"Please Andy, don't do that. Don't look at me. It is not nice."

He grinned into her face and with his mouth only pinned her head to the tatami in a hard kiss. She responded as hungrily, but her body squirmed away as his fingers sought the slit between her legs. He drew back, panting with frustration.

She said "I am ashamed that you look at me."

"We're going round the world!" he said. Again he kissed her and again she responded. He rolled her onto her stomach. She tried to roll back, the movement of her legs exposing tips of pubic hair to him. He slid the blade of his hand down the crease between her buttocks. His little finger felt the puckered button of her anus. He pushed in slightly against the clenched muscles, then moved on, dipped for a moment into the warm wet welcoming hole between her lower lips.

For a moment they stayed like that, one of his hands on a full mound, the other in the crease between them. With an inarticulate cry he pushed himself forward. His knees spread her thighs. He lay down full-length upon her, driving the breath from her lungs as he drove his tumescent cock into the softness of her waiting cunt.

"Oh please, please, Andy-san," she called. "Please please."

He withdrew for a moment and she turned a puzzled face to him. His own face was flushed and close to hers, his eyes glaring. He felt with his hand for the higher opening. She tried to squirm away again but was held by his weight and hand. He pierced her anal defense with a rigid finger, and to his surprise, the muscles made no assault on the probing digit.

"Lipstick, lipstick," she murmured.

He looked around until he could spot her purse. A second's one-handed fumbling found it. He removed the cap and applied the lipstick to her rear bud. As soon as he was finished she started struggling again, but this time he gave her no pause. His stiff penis disappeared through her anal ring until his belly rested flush against her buttocks.

He pulled out, then shoved in again. She squeaked gently "I am ashamed."

He pulled out completely and without pausing redirected his member to her vagina. She sagged against the *tatami*, and again he withdrew and pressed into her ass. She welcomed him with a small sigh. He alternated between holes, his movements speeding up.

"Not too soon," she begged. "Not too quick."

By now her cries fell on deaf ears. The instant he peaked, his entire weight poured his boiling essence into her behind.

The waves gradually subsided until he was left limp, her body panting beneath him.

He was suddenly conscious of a pain on his belly. Her hands had raked multiple parallel scratches into his skin. He loosened her wrists. She rolled over to her side, then rose gracefully to her feet.

"You have *ofuro?*"

"Yes, there's a bath." He got up, showed her the bathroom and provided a towel. She squatted on the small plastic seat and began rinsing herself with the spray from the shower head. He looked at her, following the movement of her fingers in and out of her cunt as the soap lathered.

He knelt beside her and spread her legs. She leaned back against the bath. He soaped the insides of her vagina, lathering his hand generously. Then with one finger he soaped inside her anus. She leaned back on the plastic stool and opened her legs to afford him an easier access. His movements quickened, directed by her own hand. Soon both of them were spotted with lather. Her breathing grew harsher and quicker. She gave off a quiver, then another. Her body arched and her teeth ground as she climaxed against their joined hands.

"Andy-san, can I be your steady?" she asked suddenly.

"What?" he exclaimed, startled by the odd question.

"Andy-san, I like to go out with you, I like you very much, and what you do . . ."

"But I . . ." he floundered.

"I don't mind, you have other girls, OK? But you will be my steady? I will come when you want me? OK?"

Without a word he nodded.

They rinsed her off and she became conscious again of his eyes as he looked at her body.

"Please Andy-san," she said as she wrapped herself with a towel. "I am ashamed. You must not look."

He did not answer, turned his back and seated himself on the small plastic stool on the floor. Soon her hands, strong and competent, were soaping his back with a small wash-cloth. The sensation of her soapy hands was relaxing and Andy, tired from his efforts, almost fell asleep. He woke as her sudsy strokes reached his belly. He winced slightly as the soap burned on the deep red scratches. She lathered the dark curls at the base of his cock and then dropped the towel.

Her fingers began playing with his cock. The slickness of her soapy hands knowingly touched the tip. Slowly, the soft penis began to tumesce and he was conscious of the warmth of her body and the points of her breasts as she leaned against his back.

The cock rose fully as her palms stroked it. His hips began to jerk and she speeded up her movements. He wanted to stop her but curiosity overcame him. She leaned over his shoulder and he tried to kiss her. Her face was so intent on what she was doing that the tongue protruding from the side of his mouth barely made contact with her ear. Suddenly he found he was no longer in control. His cock jerked once, then again. The relief as he came was accompanied by pain as the last drops of semen made their way through his penis. The driblets of come whitened the dark reddish brown crown of his cock, as white as the lather of the soap below.

She gave a sigh as she saw his come emerge. "It is the first time I have *seen* that," she said. Her eyes were intent as the final jerks of his penis ended. "It always happens inside me, you see."

An idea occurred to him. "Sip it," said Andy.

"But there is soap on it!" she objected, again in that babydoll voice that made him want to force her.

"Not on the head," he said. "Just lick the jizm. Leave the soap," he added generously then put a hand on her head as he turned on the stool to face her, and pushed her head down.

She bent before him and held the cock in her hand with only the helmet-shaped head showing. He looked at her smooth, blocky back as she looked at the member. Its single eye stared back blind with his emissions. He rose to his feet and tilted her head back. She brought her lips to the wet knob and her lips extended. She sipped delicately. The salty, sour taste of his sperm touched her tongue. She wet her lips, then licked the end of his cock voraciously. The white stringy drops disappeared and she looked up at him, smiled, and rose to her feet. Her arms went about his neck and she presented her lips to his. Her tongue delved deeply into the warmth of his mouth and they stood, slick and soapy body to body, for a long moment.

At last the kiss broke. She bent down and picked up the plastic bucket and sluiced him down, then herself. Rivulets of water ran down her slick brown skin. He climbed into the high sided *furo* bath and sat down. The water rose to his chest. She stepped in after him and he stopped her, one foot over the edge. His fingers probed into her cunt, frigging her little clitoris. Her face was impassive as he led her into the hot water. The water rose to his chin; he stood as she immersed herself. She looked up at him, and the sight of her red pursed lips was too much. He pushed forward with his soft, exhausted prick. She raised a hand to his crotch but he brushed it aside. Passively, she opened her mouth and he inserted the shrivelled member with his fingers. It lay there on her tongue. Then she closed her lips and sucked it in. She began to work, her eyes screwed up at him. Notwithstanding her efforts, his tired member refused to respond. But the softness of the cock in her mouth urged her on, and for him, the pleasure of actually feeling her mouth work on him without the urgency of an erection was pleasurable.

When he withdrew and sank into the water with her, he decided he had found a new pleasure. She nestled comfortably in his arms until the water cooled and drove them both out.

CHAPTER 7:
Double Gold

Routine, particularly after overcoming a difficulty, always paled on Jim quickly. He wondered where Andy was. His roommate still had not returned from his errands. Jim shied from thinking of Andy as his brother. The relationship, with one who was similar in an eerie way and yet different, made him uneasy. Andy's bed was rumpled and obviously used, but the man himself was gone. Jim grinned to himself. At least in the bed department they seemed well matched. He played a computer game for a while, then when that ceased to entertain him, thought of calling up someone, preferably female, and found he knew hardly anyone. He had purposely not taken any steps to contact Chieko, and Michiko Teraoka limited her visits; otherwise, his social contacts were minimal.

He descended to the street. Left would take him to Aoyama, and the downtown centers of Shibuya or Shinjuku, slightly lower-class and studentish. Right would lead to Roppongi, with its frenetic nightlife and discos and foreign-inspired atmosphere. He tossed a mental coin, then took the first cab. Roppongi it was.

Jim stood with his back to Almond, the coffeehouse at

Roppongi intersection and watched the crowds pass by. Tinkling little girls, some not so little, and some pretending to be little. Teenyboppers, teenagers, and respectable wives waited for their boy- or girlfriends, husbands, lovers, and friends before Almond. The crowd was heavily laced with *gaijin* of all colors and sizes and both sexes. Jim thought about food: there was a pub nearby which served real T-bone steaks. . . . It occurred to him to try a disco: loud music, free snacks, girls to look at, and who knows. . . . "Leopard," which he fancied, was near the intersection and he rode the lift to the fifth floor. Through the lobby he emerged into the mirrored walls, colored flashing lights and movement of the disco. But the minute he stepped in, he knew he had made a mistake. Melancholy was in full swing now, and he regarded the dancing couples, groups, and singles with distaste.

They were dancing together, admiring their own motions in the full-length mirror, ignoring everyone else. Jim admired their movements. One was shorter than the other and a bit plumper. Her ass stretched the fabric of her jeans and he wondered how she got into them. She wore a sheer bra and blouse and Jim could see her erect nipples, dark under the fabric.

The taller one wore her hair in a ponytail. She danced jerkily. Her leotard top revealed a pair of full breasts without a bra. Her face was doll-like and expressionless, with a small mouth and straight nose.

The music slowed and they clasped one another tightly. A young man asked one of them to dance, and they both turned him down with looks of scorn.

Jim watched them for an hour. During that time they left the dance floor only to eat and drink. Several times men approached them, *gaijin* as well as Japanese and asked one or the other, or both, to dance. They were rejected each time. Jim danced now and again, then finally found himself sitting next to one of them as they consumed cokes and crackers. They were murmuring to one another, and their lips were wet. The thinner blonde had a wallet tucked into the back pocket of her jeans. He extracted it without difficulty. While they danced, he riffled through it.

"Do your parents know you are lovers?" he asked pleasantly, only mildly intrigued, when they sat down beside him again. Both stared at Jim. "If not," he added, "you shouldn't carry such revealing pictures."

"Are you a detective?" said the plumper one.

"Are you going to tell them?" The taller one was in obvious distress, but controlling herself. "Please don't!? I'll do anything. I'll pay you . . ."

Jim looked at them for a moment. Their panic was outside his comprehension. He shrugged, then rose to go. He was outside the disco waiting for the elevator, when he heard steps behind him. The two blondes approached. Something in their eyes spoke trouble, and Jim regretted having poked his nose into their affairs. He saw the glint in one blonde's fist, and his reflexes took over. He had twitched the switchblade away from her before she knew it was gone.

"Are you crazy?" he asked.

She breathed heavily in his grip as the elevator arrived. They followed him into the elevator, and he found he could not let go of the girl.

"Stop it Mandy!" the plumper one urged. Then "Are you taking us back home?"

Jim sighed. "Let's talk about it, huh? I don't mean you any harm . . ."

They hung their heads. Mandy looked at the other one and licked her lips, then back at him. "Maybe, . . . Maybe if we . . . Joanie? Please can't we . . . My parents will kill me if they find out!"

Joanie, the plumper blonde nodded, her eyes fixed on

Jim's. Somehow, they were all in the rear seat of a taxi as Jim was giving directions to the cabby. He stroked both blond heads as their hands went to his crotch, and kneaded his growing cock through his pants. "When we reach home," he whispered to them. They relaxed against him, their hands joined over the bulge in his pants. He hoped Andy was away, and then the thought occurred to him that it might be fun if his partner and/or brother were there. They hadn't shared girls yet.

He sat on the couch and looked at them gravely as they stood before him. "This is new to you?" he asked, pointing to his erect cock. It stood up from his fly, the black hairs framing the base.

Mandy and Joanie nodded together.

"Then I'm going to fuck you both," he said directly. "It's only fair, in return for trying to kill me."

"I was afraid," said Mandy shyly.

"Afraid of what?" asked Jim. He thought he knew the answer, but wanted to hear it from her own cherry-red lips.

"That we . . . that we . . ." Joanie, the plumper one stuttered.

"That I'd tell the world you're lesbians?" he asked gently. They nodded again. "Have you ever had a man?" he asked.

"No. Yes." The words came in unison. Joanie had not; Mandy had.

"I didn't like it," she confessed. "He fumbled all over inside me with his fingers. It wasn't pleasant at all. Then he shoved his thing into me . . ."

"Prick."

"What?" she asked, startled.

"Prick. Its called a prick, or cock, or penis," Jim supplied.

"Yes. Anyway, he shoved it inside me, and I didn't like it."

"Maybe he just didn't know how," said Jim. "I do. Here, why don't you make his acquaintance."

Shyly, somewhat reluctantly, they touched the velvety surface. They gained more confidence as their hands joined, and they explored the length of the dark shaft. At last Joanie, the more adventurous of the two, knelt before him. She licked the tip reluctantly, then spat out the transparent drop of liquid that had touched her lip. "Ugh, horrible."

"Not at all," said Jim breathing deeply. "Surely you've licked Mandy? Didn't that taste good?"

"Yes," she said shyly, coloring.

"Do it again," he ordered.

The pink tongue licked out again, and then, bravely, she slipped the head between her lips and sucked tentatively.

"Lovely," he sighed.

Mandy held the shaft and stroked it gently, intent on her friend's actions. Joanie gradually grew bolder. Her blond hair bobbed as she sucked at the growing shaft. "My jaw is tired," she announced at last, pulling away.

"How about you, Mandy?" Jim asked, waving his tool in her direction. It was fully engorged and shiny from Joanie's oral ministrations.

"Yes, you have to. I did it," said the plumper girl.

Reluctantly Mandy knelt and started sucking. As her mouth engulfed the head, she tried to pull away. Jim quickly grabbed her pony tail and forced her mouth downwards. "You were going to knife me, remember?" Joanie knelt and put her arms around her friend, one hand stroking her full breast. She kissed the pink cheek and whispered "Do it Mandy, it's OK." She kissed again, and Mandy bravely sucked at the shaft of warm flesh.

The juices rose in Jim's groin and he knew he had to pull away. Mandy raised her head and licked her lips. Both pairs of blue eyes stared into his own. "I think I'd like a show,"

Jim said. "Why don't you undress. No, actually, why don't
we start with Joanie while Mandy and I watch?"

He pulled the taller blonde down by his side. The other
posed for a moment before them. She ran her hands over her
thighs, then stroked her belly. For a moment she cupped her
breasts, pinching the nipples softly, then harder. Jim noted
that for future reference. Joanie's fingers went to the buttons
of her blouse, and she undid them one by one. She shrugged
out of the silk and her hands moved to her back.

"No! Wait. Come here, Joanie," Mandy begged.

Joanie turned around obligingly. Mandy and Jim stood up.
Mandy undid the bra hooks, then kissed the smooth flesh,
lined with the bra marks. Jim slid his hands under her armpits
and held her breasts which seemed to expand in his palms.
He drew the reluctant Mandy back as the bra dropped to the
floor and Joanie turned around. Her breasts were relatively
flat with dark pink nipples and large aureoles. Mandy leaned
forward and kissed each breast. Jim explored Mandy's
body through her clothes, rubbing his hard cock against
the covered crease of her ass. He pulled her back to the
sofa.

Joanie stood for a moment, then unzipped her jeans. She
was wearing pink sheer panties which emphasized the smooth
blondness of her pubic hair. She turned around again, in
silence, and dropped the pants. Turning back, her hand dipped
into her panties. Through the pink material Mandy and Jim
could see her cupping her mound, fingering herself. Then she
bent over and turned in one movement, showing them her
hanging breasts and the smooth white expanse of her backside. Both Jim and Mandy were breathing heavily. The slim
girl rose from her seat and embraced her nude companion.
Her lips rested on her friend's until Jim broke their embrace.
He hugged Mandy. His mouth covered her reluctant lips, and
he kissed her lovingly. Then he drew Joanie's naked form to

him and kissed her deeply as well. Her tongue, unlike her friend's, responded to his ardently. They explored one another's mouths, her tongue flicking against his own. He drew her down beside him to the couch, while Mandy stood center stage.

She looked at them, delaying her actions while Jim stroked Joanie's firm skin. His hands pinched her nipples gently, and he insinuated a hand between her thighs, which opened with expectation. Mandy began her strip. She unbuttoned her jeans first, then lowered the pants to the ground. Standing a second before them, she raised her hands to her top.

"Turn on the stereo," suggested Jim. In her leotard, she searched among the tapes until she found an appropriate cassette. She began an inexpert bump and grind, then slid out of the top of the black stretch fabric. Her nipples were erect, tiny pink buds on firm strong breasts. She worked the black cloth to the floor, exposing a perfectly rounded belly and an enormous bush of dark golden hair that ran almost from her belly button to her thighs. The fabric dropped and Mandy closed her eyes as she swayed to the music. The fluffy bush hid all signs of her lower lips which she brushed occasionally with her hand.

"You're so beautiful, Mand!" exclaimed the plumper girl. Jim could barely contain his excitement. His hands dug under Joanie's ass and he hauled her onto his lap. She straddled him, staring intently at Mandy who was dancing languidly to the music. Urged by his hands, Joanie raised her ass to him. His stiff cock nosed about for a few seconds, then he found the soft opening. She slid down on it easily.

Mandy looked at the couple before her. The dark, Japanese-looking man and the plump girl on his knees. Joanie's eyes were closed and her head was tilted to one side as she responded to Jim's mouth on her neck. Her hands stroked the man's thighs. Between her parted legs Mandy could see the

erect shaft that disappeared into the full pink lips she loved to
play with. The shaft emerged and the ball bag underneath
moved sinuously. The cock, wet and slick looking, emerged
again and Mandy found herself riveted to the sight.

Jim opened his eyes and motioned her towards them. She
knew instinctively what was wanted. Slowly she nuzzled
Joanie's neck and throat, meeting Jim's probing tongue reluctantly. She descended lower, drawn by the vision she had
seen. Joanie's nipples came in for a thorough laving, and she
found she had to beg with her tongue to be allowed access to
them from between Jim's strong fingers. They parted at last
and each nipple in turn was subject to Mandy's delicate
kisses. She saw how the man's fingers excited her friend,
pinching the saliva-coated nubbins harshly, something she
had always wished to do yet never dared.

Her lips continued downwards, and she tongued her friend's
navel, making her wriggle and pulse at the touch. Then
finally she reached the blonde bush. She was breathing heavily by the time her mouth rested on Joanie's pubis. Jim and
Joanie were almost still, the sole movement a pulsing of their
bodies as little tingles of pleasure ran through them. Mandy
knew it was up to her. Love of her friend and a desire to be
the source of her pleasure flooded through her. She licked
Joanie's fat clitoris, pushing her face deep between the two
pairs of thighs, one smooth, the other muscular and hairy.
She licked and sucked with abandon now, her energies directed at the pleasure of her lover. But the long shaft, sticky
with Joanie's juices, took its share of attention, and for a
fleeting moment Mandy wondered what it would be like
swelling and spurting in her mouth. The pulsations of the two
figures grew stronger. She licked deeper and harder, trying to
share the pleasure of her friend's cunt with the stiff pole that
filled it. She could barely hear the gasps and sounds of the
two above her, wrapped as she was entirely in the damp

darkness between their thighs. Her fingers moved between her own legs, exciting herself too, to a climax the others were not far from reaching.

The cock seemed to swell against the flat of her tongue. Jim's muscles tensed and he shoved his shaft deeper into Joanie. Mandy felt a stream pulse through the shaft. It passed her by in jerk after jerk of the pole. Froth began to emerge from Joanie's cunt as her thighs contracted in orgasm.

Jim looked down at the slimmer girl on her knees before them. Joanie was stroking her friend's face. Her mouth was open and her eyes half shut. Mandy looked up at them tiredly, but with pride. Her face was wet with perspiration—theirs and hers—and with the residue of their juices which had smeared her pale cheeks. Jim drew her up to him and kissed her deeply. This time she responded and he could taste the mixed flavor of his discharge and Joanie's juices. Joanie licked her friend's cheek, then took her face in both her hands and kissed her. "That was the best, Mand. The upper super best." The two girls kissed again, their hairs mingling in a damp tangle.

Joanie disengaged from Jim reluctantly and sank down beside her friend. They examined Jim's cock critically. Mandy leaned forward and sniffed. "It smells like you do, Joanie," she said. Then her tongue licked out and laved the plum tip.

"It's your turn now, Mand," Joanie prompted.

"Lie on your back, here on the sofa," Jim commanded. Joanie stepped back and helped Jim spread her friend's warm golden thighs. They examined Mandy's bush in silence. Mandy stared back at the two intent faces.

"I've never seen this," Joanie confessed. "We always make love in the dark."

Mandy's mound of light brown curls were fluffy, down-like. Jim ran his hands through the luxuriant growth and Joanie's fingers joined him. Jim slipped away and Joanie continued the stroking, whispering endearments as she did so. Jim knelt by the supine blond's side and showed her the hairbrush. She drew back involuntarily and was soothed again by her friend. Jim started brushing the curls, imparting a sheen to them. The soft bristled brush approached Mandy's cunt lips and she shivered in anticipation. Her hips started to respond to the movements of the brush as her clitoris and the sensitive flesh around it were brushed delicately by Jim, then stroked by Joanie.

The stroking continued and Mandy's eyes closed. Joanie stopped, and Mandy wished she would continue. She heard a whisper, and then Joanie's hands were reapplied to her bush while the brush stroked at the fur between her thighs. Her lower lips were on fire now, the bristles having sensitized the lips to a degree she had never felt before. Joanie's hands were now soothing and slick, and opening her eyes, Mandy saw that her friend's fingers were coated with a hair gel. Mandy smiled dreamily and her insides surged in a minor climax which she made no effort to hide. As Jim sucked on her nipple, she raised the full mound for his approval. All fear of him was gone now. Joanie took the brush and shaped the vast bush while Jim applied himself to Mandy's breasts and mouth. Now she responded ardently to his kisses, sticking her tongue into his mouth, exploring his body with her hands, pulling at his cock. She found the silky shaft to be a plaything rather than the instrument of pain she had experienced before. She pulled him to her mouth while the stroking of her pussy continued. Obligingly, Jim knelt over her face. She explored his scrotum with her lips and tongue, mouthing each of his eggs in turn. He arched her head back and her lips parted, knowing what was to come.

The spongy head of his cock met her lips and she opened her mouth with welcome. Sucking the shaft in was easy and she found that she could pull in more and more of the fleshy stick. It butted the entrance to her throat and she found she could relax the muscles and allow its access. She breathed through her nose until his hairy balls rested on her forehead. He pulled back and she manipulated the shaft in and out of her mouth while her cheeks hollowed hungrily. The pressure in her loins was growing and her hips and mouth pulsed with the same rhythm. Jim pulled out of her which she allowed regretfully, conscious of the wonderful feel of the male shaft as it slid between her lips.

"Sit up, Mandy," Joanie whispered encouragingly.

They all examined Mandy's pussy. Joanie provided her compact mirror. She had sculpted the fur into a coiffure of elaborate ringlets and swirls. Each hair was in place.

"You have a great future as a hair stylist," Jim said. His cock was stiff and slick, and he pushed Mandy back onto the sofa. She fell back expectantly and he climbed between her legs. She cried out with pleasure as she felt the long warm shaft slide between her lips and enter deep into her. Her thighs clamped over Jim's behind and she pulled Joanie to her mouth. They fumbled about while Jim pumped steadily into her until Joanie was riding her lover's active mouth. Jim applied his mouth to Joanie's ass, dipping into the crack between her buns, occasionally finding Mandy's eager tongue as well. The tempo increased and both girls yowled as Jim poured his boiling sperm deep into Mandy's willing cunt. His cock jerked fiercely and Mandy rose to meet it, almost unsaddling Joanie in the process.

They collapsed together in a heap, stroking one another and dipping into the residues that covered both cunts and Jim's cock. Finally, they dressed.

"I wish I had a present to give you," Jim said.

"A present?" Joanie asked in surprise. "Why?"

"Something very special," he smiled. "A *harigata*."

"What's that?" Mandy asked.

"A cock. You tie it around your waist and fuck Joanie."

She chuckled, easily this time. "We don't need that. Besides, if we feel we need a cock, we can have you, right?"

"Besides," Joanie sniffed, "I wouldn't want any piece of rubber shoved into me."

Jim shook his head. "A present, I said. Not cheap rubber. Ivory or jade. You'll love it."

He walked them to the door.

"What the hell was that?" Andy asked as he stepped into the apartment, staring down the corridor at the two retreating blonde backs. "Why didn't you wait for me?"

"No time," said Jim. "Best two . . . What's the matter?" He saw the look on Andy's face.

Wordlessly, Andy handed him a letter. His hand trembled slightly and the onionskin paper rustled in his hand. "Just read the important parts. Here . . ." He pointed.

"Dear Andy . . . hmm skip all that ah, yes . . .

. . . I know how much all that has bothered you. You know that for us you are our eldest brother, no matter what. However, I did what you said and I checked up on Mary Typhon. First, there aren't many Typhons beyond some families in Europe (see how good my information is? That's what happens when I go out with a demographer!! And boy, is he something!!! Well, anyway . . .). I found her records at the Santa Barbara General hospital and managed to trace them. First, be ready for a shock. She had not one baby, but two: twins, Andrew and James (so now you've got another brother: Sammy, by the way, is going to be class valedictorian). Father unknown, or at least she didn't put it down. There are no records I could find for James. Much love, Rhonda"

Jim reread the paragraph and lowered the letter slowly. "That can't be," he said steadily. "Look, notwithstanding all the features we share and everything, *I'm* obviously at

least part Japanese. You are not. It just can't be. Two mothers I could buy, but one mother and two fathers? And twins?
It can't be!''

Andy shook his head. "It is. I don't know how, but it is.
We're twins all right, from the same mother. Different fathers. There's something else, too. I'm being followed.''

Jim frowned. Andy raised a hand and added "I know it
sounds crazy, but I am," he insisted.

"I wasn't going to say you aren't," Jim replied. "I had the
same feeling. Remember what happened in Kabukicho? That
was pretty odd, and I think I've seen the guy again. . . .''

They looked at one another. "What the *hell* is going on?"

CHAPTER 8:
The Bard's Tongue

The knock on the door disturbed Andy at work. It was early afternoon and not a time for visitors. He swore, stretched, and stumped across the apartment to the door. His head was full of figures. He liked economics, but columns of figures bored him.

"Excuse me, I am Mrs. Akabane. This is my daughter, Sumiko. I live in the neighborhood. I am very sorry to disturb you . . ."

She was rather tall for a Japanese, and thinner than he liked. Dressed formally in high heels and dark stockings she looked even taller. She held a large bow-wrapped package. Hovering beside her was a teenage girl, her hair in a ponytail. She was nearing eighteen, and obviously the woman's daughter.

Andy shrugged mentally. "Please come in."

"I am so sorry to disturb you."

The two women sat first on the mat, for politeness sake. When he insisted, they moved to the *zabuton* cushions he had spread for them.

"It is so kind of you to let me bother you like this," the mother said. The teenager's eyes were darting about the room, trying to assess the occupant. Her eyes fell on the record collection, wondering if Andy were some stodgy Westerner with Beethoven on the brain. She slumped in her seat, her skirt tucked neatly under her. She had wanted to come in jeans and the colorful sweatshirt which said "SEXWAX: It's Good For Your Stick" which was all the rage. She wasn't sure she understood what it meant, but *gaijin* seemed to glance at her with approval. She listened with a sour face to her mother. Mr. Mid-laa was a handsome man, slightly old, of course, and with the odd face of a *gaijin*. She thought he would have had possibilities if he hadn't had to fulfill this hateful role.

"Midlaa-san," Mrs. Akabane said formally. "I am sorry to trouble you, but I have seen you going to work often. We have also been on the train together. Please. I must ask you to help me."

Andy bowed and said properly "Anything whatsoever."

Encouraged, she plunged on. "My daughter is soon to be eighteen. She is in her last year in high school. Soon she must enter college. But her English is terrible. Please can you help?"

From experience, Andy knew what to expect. He cursed inwardly. He would have liked to respond favorably, but his English-teaching days—something most *gaijin* did as a matter of course—were over. At least he had hoped so.

"Akabane-san, I would like to help, but I do not teach English . . ."

"Please Mr. Mid-laa. I know this is a great imposition. We have tried a preparatory school, but my stupid daughter was not successful there. If she is to enter college, she must have help . . ."

"I realize that but. . . ."

Andy tried every means he could to avoid the task. He pleaded work, inexperience, lack of composure, and more work. The average individual would have taken the hint and been off. Not so the *kyoiku mama;* an "education mother" to the core. Mrs. Akabane would only withdraw with his full capitulation. Which she got. Eventually.

"Serves you right for looking like a proper *gaijin,*" laughed Jim. "When is the little terror coming?"

"Tomorrow, in bobby socks and sailor suit no doubt." Andy shuddered at the image of the high school girl, in the standard blue sailor uniform. At least she wasn't male. *They* dressed in high collar mao jackets and were universally sullen and pimply.

Half an hour into the first lesson Andy found himself drenched in sweat. He wondered how his friends were able to stand teaching the whole day. Sumiko was still looking at him with every sign of attention, but he knew it was a sham. No high school student could possibly be so stupid. She could not repeat a proper English sentence twice running, nor compose a question that made any sense. He chewed his lip for awhile as she looked at him with an opaque gaze. Her mother had said "by any means possible"? Well, there must be some other means . . . His eye lit on the stack of records.

"What kind of music do you like?" His question startled her. "John Denver," she said. The answer was the first spontaneous response he had gotten from her. He pointed to the stereo.

"Go choose one of the records. There are two of his albums there."

She rose smoothly. She put the album on, louder than he liked, and sat down again.

"Do you understand the words?"

"Yes," she said, then reconsidered and added shyly "Not really Midlaa-sensei . . ."

Andy nodded. Most Japanese could read English, a few could even write, after a fashion, but the school system was not really designed to teach the language and many English teachers were not fluent in it themselves. They taught the students by rote, and the subsequent lack of interest and failure in understanding the foreign tongue was no surprise.

Her hand was close to his. She stroked the back of it so lightly it would not have intruded on his consciousness but for the fact that it was done in his full sight. For a moment he considered removing his hand; then the mother's look and her entreaty came to him again. Sumiko *must* pass her exams. He thought of a way of reinforcing her behavior. As she repeated the words with proper pronunciation, he would press his hand against hers. When she made a mistake, or plead ignorant about the meaning of words or sentences, he would withdraw his hand.

Soon he discovered that reinforcement has two disadvantages. First, to be effective the stimulus had to be increased. She was soon pressing her thigh against his, and her hand was inching its way into lengthy strokes of his arm to his shoulder.

Second, the stimulus was soon stimulating him. Before long, there was a large tense bulge distending his pants. It was not at first noticeable under the table, but it also meant he was trapped where he was.

"I am hot!" she announced as the record ended. Then, "Aren't you going to change it?"

"Not quite yet," Andy answered. He was damned if he was going to parade his erection before this chippy.

She smiled, rose, and replaced the record. Repeating, "I am hot," she removed her sailor-suit jacket. Under her sheer T-shirt she obviously wore no bra. Her breasts were not prominent, but the nipples and the aureolae merged in conicle tips. She let her jacket drop and her shoulder slumped as she regarded him from under her disarranged hair.

"Andy-san, you do not like me?"

He moved uncomfortably, and she walked around the table to sit back on her cushion. She caught sight of the bulge in his pants. Her eyes widened and she squealed "Oh, you do, you do!" and reached for his crotch.

The next few moments were a confusion of groping, flying clothes and squeals of delight from the girl. They were both stripped but for socks before Andy could figure out quite what to do about it. She grasped his erect penis with familiarity and led him to his bedroom by it.

Sumiko lay on the bed and spread her legs as wide as she could. He felt her wet cunt gently. Impatiently she reached for his hand and pulled him down to her. "Now, now, do it."

He pulled away. "Wait. . . . Isn't this your first time?"

"Yes, of course. That's why I want you to do it to me, right now!"

He laughed as she pulled him to her again and tried to eel her way under his body. "I'd rather prepare you first, you know, play with you a bit . . ."

"We've played enough. *I*'ve played enough. Now I want the real thing." She pulled at his cock. She was warm and smooth under him, her breasts almost unnoticeable. He kissed her deeply once, and then she turned her face aside, concentrating on fumbling with his cock. Finally, she found the entrance to her hole with its tip. He moved his lips lightly. Feeling the end of the shaft at the sensitive entrance to her vagina she said "Aah. Now push it in."

He pushed and felt a slight resistance. She urged him on, her arms around his shoulders, her lips now seeking his. Andy pushed again and broke into her. She gasped with pain, and through clenched teeth said "Go on, go on." Andy pushed himself deeper, the channels of her virgin cunt yielding reluctantly to the male member. At last he felt the hairs of their crotches merging. She pushed at his chest. Misunderstanding, he started to pull out.

"No, no," Sumiko whined. "Stay inside. Raise your chest."

Andy did as he was told. He felt her hand between their bodies. She felt for his root and its descent into her depths. She touched the slickness there, smearing it on her fingers, then brought her hand to her face. The tips of the fingers were touched with spots of blood. Sumiko smiled with pride.

"I am not a virgin anymore, then."

Andy jogged his rump and she closed her eyes, abandoning herself to the occasion. The tightness of a virgin cunt was a sensation he had never felt before. She stretched and contracted her arms around him, feeling all over his body. Each movement was one of discovery, and as the tide of pleasure mounted in her, she surrendered herself to her own sensations. She panted and squealed her delight as he puffed over her, nipping her flat nipples with his teeth and sucking her breasts alternately into his mouth. The climax rose in her and she whimpered in its approach. Her mouth formed an O, pink rimmed and dark centered. Rasping sounds came from her throat and a tiny thread of spittle ran from the corner of her mouth. She clutched him convulsively and Andy spewed his load in fiery rushes that accentuated her own orgasm.

She pushed him off too soon, weary of his weight, then sat up to examine herself and then him. His cock was now a shriveled red morsel, and she looked at it curiously, perplexed that such a tiny instrument could give her such pleasure. She touched a finger to her cunt, overflowing with his spunk and her own juices. Her nose wrinkled when she smelled the fluids and she wiped her fingers on the sheet.

"Did you like it?" he interrupted her explorations.

"Oh Andy-san. It was wonderful. Wonderful. Why do adults keep things like this for themselves?"

"Too good for the young," he said with a smile. "Look at you, it could have gone on much longer. . . ."

"There are many things I have to learn," she said. Her eyes were bright and calculating.

The thought of what Mrs. Akabane would say if she knew what he was teaching her daughter instead of English ran through Andy's brain. Then the practical side took over. Suppose his English teaching was successful? Suppose . . .

"Sumiko," he said forcefully. "You are here to learn English."

Her face turned sullen.

"Learn English you shall. At the end of every lesson we will have some fun. *If* you've been good. If you've actually improved, I shall also teach you other things. As a reward."

She grinned suddenly. The idea caught her fancy. "What other things?"

"Well, . . . Like this." He rose suddenly, bent over her, and licked her bloody cunt. The blood tasted awful, but he knew he had to stimulate her interest. Her hips jerked in surprise and she made a sound deep in her throat. "Is it a deal?" he asked, peering into her eyes.

"Yes, yes of course. You must not tell though. I will be the best student you have ever had. But you must also teach me the English for these things," as she held his cock as softly as she could in her palms. He grinned.

CHAPTER 9:
The Dream of Chuan-tzu

Jim rode from the Waseda stop, past Gaigodai and north-wards into the residential zone near Ikegawa University. He always enjoyed riding the streetcar, one of the last in Tokyo. He liked the smell of old oil, and the sense of slow travel put him at ease. Finding an address in Tokyo is a problem. Houses are not numbered sequentially, and few of them have the number displayed in any case. Streets have no names nor numbers.

The policeman in the police box was helpful, particularly when he saw Michiko Teraoka's note, which Jim had made sure to secure. Nonetheless, he checked Jim's alien registration card. A greater shock awaited him, and he had to fight to keep his face from giving himself away. The house was owned by a Mr. Kitamura, but had not been occupied by him for many years. Nonetheless, with a faint hope, Jim knocked on the door.

The inner door slid open and he heard a female voice call out *"Dozo,* please come in."

Jim opened the outer door and stepped into the pebble-paved *genkan*. A young woman, her hair dyed a carroty yellow was peering at him over square, old-fashioned spectacles. She held a book in her hands.

"Excuse me, housewife," Jim said.

She interrupted him brusquely. "'I'm not the housewife.'"

"Excuse me," he bowed, then, trying to recoup, added in English "Excuse me, my Japanese is not so good."

"Oh, you are a foreigner?" she said and smiled suddenly. "I am sorry for being rude, I did not know."

"No, no. I am sorry for disturbing you. My name is Jim Suzuki. I would like some help if I may."

"Of course, anything at all. Won't you come up?" She backed into the house. He shed his shoes and followed, wondering about her openness: the *genkan* was designed to keep unwanted visitors at a polite distance without entering the house itself.

They entered a typical student room. Snowdrifts of paper lay everywhere. Books were piled on a desk and chair in a corner, on shelves, on the *tatami* mats. The girl's clothes, nylons and sweaters were climbing on and buried under the books like marine life caught in a sea quake. She sat before a low, littered Japanese table and motioned him to a *zabuton* cushion on the mat near her. As he sat he was conscious of her calculating look as she gauged his height. Her eyes travelled over him like a stockman investigating the qualities of a steer.

"My name is Yoko. Where are you from?"

"California," he said and grinned. A popular place among trendy young Japanese.

"You are Japanese. That is," she foundered "A *nisei?*"

"Yes," Jim said. "And perhaps you can help me. I am looking for a relative. A Mr. Kitamura who used to live here. This is still his house, I believe . . ."

She shook her head. "No, no. A Mr. Sato bought it some years ago. I rent this room; others live in other rooms. I do not recall . . . Well, maybe . . . I'm not sure." Notwithstanding her verbal confusion, Jim sensed there was less ignorance in her mind than she displayed.

"Perhaps something could remind you? Or you know something about the former owner?"

"No. No. . . ." Yoko said slowly. Her carroty hair shook.

"Could I call you? Perhaps later you might recall . . ."

"I'll tell you what," she said. "We are having a party. I belong to a conversation circle. Perhaps you would care to come? This evening? By then I might remember . . ."

Jim sighed to himself. "Conversation Circles" were the "in" thing for aspiring English students. Bringing a real live *gaijin* was a feather in any member's hat. Otherwise, the members sat around and criticized each other's English. A malicious thought occurred to him. "Could I bring a friend? A foreigner too, from New York?"

"Of course!" she beamed.

"The little calculating bitch thought it all out," said Jim in rueful admiration. He and Andy were dressed in suits, heading for Ikegawa University on the tram. "She wanted to present some foreigners to her damn English circle, and we're it."

"Who we, Kemo-sabe? Why you no go alone into danger?"

"Why should I suffer alone, Tonto?" Jim retorted. Through the window he could see a mass of orange hair waiting at the stop. She wasn't leaving anything to chance.

The party was not as bad as Jim had expected. There was decent food, dancing, and a few pretty girls, though Yoko took care to monopolize her catches as well as she could. She wore a mini that showed rather thin legs, and a tight sweater to the envy of her female peers and the delight of the males.

There were some other foreigners there, at least two of whom were known to Jim personally. One was a young Englishman with fair hair and a long nose whom Jim recalled seeing at the Foreign Student Office. It took Jim a long time to remember his name—Harvey—and a much shorter time to forget it.

The other was an American named Lynette. Some people, Jim had long decided, simply got on his nerves for no obvious reason, and this girl was one. It was probably her behavior. With whey-colored skin, she had large breasts and an open, even attractive face. But she acted the American abroad with a vengeance, and Jim was Japanese enough to feel insulted.

"Hey, this is some dull party," she said. "But I guess all the Japanese parties I've been to are like this." Jim glanced over to where Yoko and Andy were deep in conversation, but no rescue came. "Let's dance," she said and moved into his arms. He tried to follow, but made himself as heavy-footed as he could. She seemed not to mind, even after he had trodden on her feet twice. Her body tried to mould itself to his, and he found himself having to fend her off. She smiled dreamily into his face. Harvey happened by, close enough to foist her off on him, but she soon hovered near Jim again.

The tail of her shirt had been raised and tied around her waist. Jim had just decided that she might be worth the effort when Yoko intervened. She cornered Jim and made it clear that she considered him to be her property. Andy looked on with amusement as Yoko clung to his brother, stroking his hair and driving her tiny breasts into his jacket.

Lynette approached him near the drinks later, and poured him a glass of beer. "I'd love a martini," she said. "Shame the Japanese can't mix them right. Do you like cocktails?"

"Of course," he said politely, but without enthusiasm.

"I'll make some for you. Where do you live?"

"Near Aoyama," he said vaguely.

She magically produced a calling card, and reluctantly he

followed suit. Torn between attraction and repulsion, the focus of his attention was yet on Yoko.

"How about tonight?" Lynette asked bluntly.

"Sorry," Jim shook his head. "Got some work . . ."

"That orange-headed floozy?" she asked, clearly annoyed.

Deciding to put her aside for a rainy day, Jim corrected her. "No, she is with my roommate. I'm just a third wheel, see? I've really got some work to do. Come by tomorrow . . ."

By the morning she would have a clearer head and be less likely to turn up, but, what the hell.

He excused himself. Yoko's eyes were upon him and he walked to her side, balancing his drink carefully.

"Have you remembered anything?" Jim asked as he led her onto the floor. Clinging to him, she said sweetly. "There is something, but I will tell you later. Here it is too noisy. Andy-san says that you live together, near Aoyama? Is it a nice place?"

"Yes," he answered, but thinking of when he and Andy might leave. "You should visit us some time."

"How about now?" she said. "I have had enough of the party. And we can talk more easily there . . ."

She liked the small apartment, insisting on a tour. "Such a large place," she said. "And it must be so warm. The old houses such as the one I live in are terribly cold. I bet you don't have to wear clothes at all in the winter in here!?"

She sat in a sling chair Andy had bought. She examined her legs, stretched out before her, and sipped delicately from the glass of whiskey Jim had poured.

"Would you like to tell us what you know?" said Andy into the silence. He was impatient with the game he thought she was playing.

She stared at the two men.

"Why do you want the information?" she wondered.

When they didn't answer, she added, "Well, I need to get *something* out of it, don't I?"

She pulled her short skirt higher up, exposing thin but shapely legs. Higher still, and they could see the top of her pantyhose and the juncture of her thighs.

"I shave, did you know? Here, let me show you." She pulled off her hose and panties and exposed a smoothly shaven mound to their gaze. "Sort of a nun in reverse, don't you see? I always test men first on the dance floor, and if they please me, I let them."

With a finger, she stroked the recesses between her smooth outer lips, then licked it, with a beatific smile.

"I love my own smell and taste," she remarked. "I'll have you first," she pointed to Jim. "You're both so alike. I wonder if the rest is the same too."

She spread her legs in invitation, resting her thighs on the chair's arms. Feeling like a teenager at his first time, Jim moved forward.

"Unzip your pants first," she giggled.

He complied and shuffled forward, his erection pointing before him. He knelt before her, and they both shuddered as he slid into her. She was tight with gluey slick insides that engulfed his cock. He fastened his mouth onto hers. Yoko moved her head aside and said breathlessly "Just fuck!"

His hips started a long in and out motion. She raised her legs and clutched him to her with her hands on his shoulders. Grasping her hips, he thrust into her harder, enjoying the smooth tightness inside her. She urged him on, with moans and grunts of satisfaction.

The chair was at an uncomfortable height, and Jim was eager to get it over with. He shook her and her orange-red hair flew in all directions. She still clung tightly when his crisis overcame him and his penis spurted into her depths.

Releasing him reluctantly, she parted her legs wide and stroked his thighs with the insides of her calves.

Jim moved away. Yoko motioned to Andy. He knelt in front of the chair as Jim had and pointed his prick at her entrance. The black hairs were coated with white drops.

"His name is Kitamura Dansuke," she said as he entered her. "He lives somewhere in the Japanese Alps, a village whose name I do not know. But he has . . . uh . . an office . . uh . . . in . . . Shinjuku . . . Oh that's good, that is very good. I think I am going to come. Yes I am very near. Harder, harder, yes, yes now some more. Squeeze my breasts . . ." She writhed and twisted in the chair, impaled by Andy's cock. But he was no longer trying to move. His own orgasm was upon him and it was all he could do to keep her twisting, gasping figure to the chair. Yoko raked her nails across his back, almost tearing his undershirt, and her hips jerked at him as if she were trying to swallow his loins whole. Her spasms died down, but she jerked electrically as Andy poured a stream of sperm into her to join that of his brother.

When she recovered, she stood up, holding her skirt carefully above her hips. "I think we can go to bed now. I'll go with you first," she said, pointing at Jim. He rose to his feet and she pulled her skirt over her head. Blouse and bra followed, though she had scant need of the latter. Her breasts were tiny, large nipples and aureolae almost the only feminine indication on her chest. Shaven smooth, she looked ghostly and bony. She slid into Andy's tired arms and kissed him hungrily. Her lips sucked at his and her tongue went deeply into his throat. "I will see you later," she murmured, as she followed Jim into his bedroom.

Half an hour later she was riding Andy wildly to a climax, her hands urging his fingers to pinch her erect nipples. Her soft cunt was overflowing with milky juice that splashed on his belly each time she descended onto him.

Yoko remained until the early hours of the morning. She had slipped wraith-like from one room to the other, emptying each man by turns. Insatiable, her elastic cunt had sucked them both dry without much dampening her own ardor. The two exhausted men sat dully in the kitchen, sipping at hot tea.

"Now what?" Jim said pensively.

"We find this Kitamura guy. He must be the key to the whole affair."

"We've been warned off him."

"Yeah, that Sato looked tough enough. I have an idea though. My ex-economics professor works occasionally for the Keidanren; maybe he can help us quietly."

"How's that?"

"A manufacturer's association. He's some kind of adviser there."

"Why the hell didn't you go to him earlier?"

"For one thing, I didn't want any strangers in on a personal problem. For another, he always gives me these horribly expensive cigars, you know, the ones in aluminum tubes? During the time I was a student I had to carry one of those fucking things around with me the whole time, to show him I appreciated his gift. I *hate* cigars." Andy shuddered.

Jim laughed. "Give them to me then. I love good tobacco."

Bleary with fatigue, Jim cursed under his breath as he went to answer the doorbell. It was early evening. Andy had gone off to try and see his former professor and Jim was trying to get an early night's rest. His day's appointments had gone by in a haze.

Lynette stood in the doorway leaning casually on the jamb. Jim's first inclination was to say "Oh no," and close the door, but he found his penis conspiring against him, rising under his sweatpants to Lynette's obvious satisfaction. Three minutes later she was straddling him in bed while he held her thighs and pulled her to him, biting her nipples gently.

When it was over, Jim changed his position and she fell over. Breathing heavily, she started to snore.

"Jesus Christ," Jim said. He heard Andy in the other room, and decided to join him. "Any more of that?" he asked, seeing Andy's coffee cup.

"Didn't want to disturb you," said his brother. "I heard you were busy."

"Yeah," Jim grunted. "And now I'm dead tired and she's snoring her head off." He helped himself to coffee. "I'm dead. First Yoko, and now her. If I don't get some sleep, I'll blow a hundred million yen project tomorrow."

"Use the sofa. Or use my bed," said Andy hospitably.

"And what will you . . . Hee hee, well, why not?" Jim grinned as the possibilities occurred to him. "Think she'll be able to tell the difference?"

"Maybe. I'm a much better lover than you . . ."

Jim snickered.

"No, seriously. I'm as horny as I was this morning. She any good?"

"So-so. Teachable, I'd guess. You owe me one."

Andy grinned. "Let's not count. Better one for all and all for one."

Andy stuck out a hand, which Jim slapped lightly. Jim watched as Andy stripped, struck again by their physical resemblance, then headed for sleep in Andy's bed.

Lynette was still snoring as Andy cuddled up to her. She turned her back, pressing her full buttocks to him. His cock rose immediately. He took his time, masturbating his hot member over her skin, rubbing it against her back, the crack of her ass and the tops of her thighs in the dark. She slept on, unaware of him.

Her back was soon covered with the shiny, tracks of his initial fluid. Andy lowered himself along her body until he covered her back like a spoon. He felt the large, soft breasts that rose and fell with her breathing, as gently as he could, not wishing her to wake yet. Unconsciously, she pillowed her head on one of his arms. With the other hand he explored the crack between her legs. It was damp, gluey with the results of her lovemaking with Jim. He pushed his hips forward, feeling his way with an extended forefinger. He found her anus and passed on, knowing such a penetration would rouse her. The entrance to her cunt was wet. He nudged the tip of his cock forward. She pushed back, still asleep, moving instinctively in the presence of the shaft. He slid inside and started moving, plunging deeper with each thrust. She stirred, though still not waking.

Lynette was dreaming of handsome strangers who were teasing her body. Now one of them, dark and curly haired with a tiny mole on his shoulder—something she had always fancied—was inside her. The sensation was intense and she woke up to find a real cock embedded in her.

"Oh, that's great, honey," she groaned softly. "Keep it coming, babe." For a long moment she could not remember the name of the man she was with. Japanese . . . no, Jim, that was it.

"Jim, honey, give it to me, all of it." She pushed her ass back at him, pleased that he had woken her as he had, sleepily enjoying his fucking. His cock became more demanding, pushing at her cunt. She licked the length of his forearm, and as her hand slid down the length of his flank, she noted its pleasant hairiness, which she had not noticed before.

He was nibbling at her neck and shoulders, then pushed himself away and lapped the length of her back. She wished he would do something else, something exciting, though she did not know what. Her own orgasm was growing slowly, while he seemed to have just started with his balls full.

He twisted suddenly and she found herself on her face. Her heavy breasts pillowed her chest uncomfortably.

"Wait a minute, lover," Lynette begged. She groped for a pillow and slipped it under her hips. He rose slightly, then plunged into her, as deep as he could reach. She grunted with the effort of bearing his weight. His fingers were scratching at her plentiful pubic hair. Eyes closed she turned her head in the dark, seeking his mouth. He thrust his tongue into her, past her sucking lips, and moved on her back. Her own juices were flowing freely now. She arched her back and tried to raise her loins, jamming her rump further into his belly. She mumbled incoherent words as her orgasm swept over her and her ass jerked backwards several times. His full weight on her body, he clutched at her hips and ground his cock deeply into her, then flooded her interior with his own fluid. They collapsed on the *futon,* breathing heavily together.

"That was great Jimmy, really great."

He mumbled a reply, his mouth full of the skin of her shoulder. Finally she shrugged him off her. They lay in the dark and she traced his face with the tips of her fingers, recalling each line, the high planes of the cheeks, the almost hooked nose. Lynette was becoming comfortable, nestling into his arms, when he rose and mumbled "Gotta pee," in a muted voice. She watched his naked figure silhouetted against the grey oblong of the door, until he was gone. The flush of the toilet was followed by a muted conversation from the next room. His roommate, probably, getting his rocks off with his fists, she thought cozily, enjoying the thought of a second man hearing her lovemaking.

"You were noisy," grinned Jim. He was lying naked on Andy's bed, his erect penis in his fist. Andy, his own flaccid, looked on with interest, wondering whether their cocks were as alike as their faces.

"Why do that?" Andy said in a low voice. "She's probably ready for another."

"Yeah, but I'm not. If I have to satisfy her again, I'll drop dead. Horny, but not able, that's me."

"Well, whatever, get out of my bed. I gotta get some sleep too."

Jim rose and walked out, his erection nodding before him. He crawled onto the *futon* with Lynette. The stiff cock nudged her side. She felt for it languidly. That was nice; he had washed for her. She liked that. Involuntarily, he moved his tool against her palm.

"Oh honey, that's real nice, but no. I gotta get some sleep. I usually can't come more than twice. Please honey? Please?"

Jim's hand was squeezing one of her bare breasts. The nipple was soft and limp. She started falling asleep and he continued rubbing himself against her.

"Listen, hon. If you gotta, then OK. But I gotta sleep, OK?"

Jim nodded in the dark, then kissed her and whispered "yes." He knelt over her, taking care to support his own weight. He brought her breasts together and masturbated against the two hillocks. She woke fully, seeing him crouch over her, and began to assist, fondling his balls and squeezing her tits together. He tried rubbing against her nipples, then began moving faster and faster in the valley between her breasts. Finally he felt his sperm rise and he jerked hard against her chest. Dribblets of sperm dripped out onto her skin. He rolled off her and grinned in the dark. She groped for a corner of the sheet and wiped herself, then cuddled into his arms and went to sleep.

Jim woke to the sound of her dressing. She smiled at him over her shoulder, then bent over to kiss his belly. "That was great lover, almost too great. You're really some hot stuff. We should do it again sometime." She pulled on her sweat-shirt and stood up. "It almost felt as if you were new each time," she giggled shyly at her own fancy and left, not noticing Jim's smile as he rolled over and went back to sleep.

CHAPTER 10:
Teragoya

For Omi Hanako the day had started badly. First her copying machine broke down just as she was preparing the leaflets for the Anti-Imperialist Campaign's Spring Offensive. Then Itagaki, had been un-communal. Though a devoted cell leader, he was prone to imbibing cheap *shochu* liquor in large amounts. Itagaki had come back to the commune from some meeting. He had apparently stopped at a corner liquor stand, and stank heavily of the potent sweet-potato liquor. Hanako, slightly ashamed of her bourgeois tendency, had just finished washing her hair which was wrapped in a dirty towel. The rest of the commune members—eight of them, three female— were out.

Seeing Hanako in her grey sweatshirt, Itagaki had leered at her. She wondered where he had spent the night. Still, he was a good-looking man, and her nipples hardened to be clearly visible through the heavy material. He licked his lips thoughtfully. When she knelt on the floor to attempt to fix her beloved copy machine he had come beside her and looked her up and down. She paid no attention. Members of the cell

were inured to surveillance within their ranks. There could be
no secrets.

She heard the sound of a zipper. From the corner of her
eye she noticed his prick spring erect from a forest of black
hairs. Then he had her shoulders and was bearing her down
onto the worn brown tatami mat.

Normally she would have offered no resistance. It was the
duty of all members of the cell to share themselves with all
others. Until this day, Itagaki had had little trouble from her.
But the smell of the liquor, and the fact that she was totally
unprepared made her resist instinctively.

Itagaki pushed her down on the mat and exposed her
breasts. His hands squeezed the brown nipples fiercely. One
hand dipped between her thighs and pushed her legs open.
She pushed up at his shoulders—a mistake—as he positioned
himself between her thighs. The tearing pain of his insertion
was worse than when she had been raped by the rival organi-
zation's goons. After all, they had played with her for a while
before mounting her, and the experience had not been all that
unpleasant.

His rigid cock tore into her dry cunt and she grunted at his
weight and the pain. She pushed against his chin and punched
his ribs, while his cock worked itself inside her. It became
easier but not pleasant.

"Get off!" she called. "Itagaki, get off, enough!"

He ignored her protests, slamming his cock deeper into
her. Then he started chewing on one of her nipples and she
went berserk with pain, hitting at him with her fists and
screaming. He raised his face in surprise and stopped his
movements.

"Shut up!" he ordered hoarsely.

"Let go of me!" She was furious. Her wet hair lay beneath
her in a wild damp mass.

"Shut up!" he said again, raising his body. His thick

member sent another message of burning pain into her and he wriggled his hips, his eyes starting to close.

"No!" the syllable burst out of her.

Itagaki slapped her face twice. Hard. "Shut up girl. In the revolution we must all play our part. This is yours now. I have been to an important operational meeting, and you are being insubordinate. If you do not understand discipline, you will suffer. Understand?"

She shivered at the word discipline. She had seen "discipline" administered, and the memory made her tremble. He took her involuntary movements as an invitation. His eyes closed and his movements speeded up. She clutched him helplessly, hoping for some pleasure. Then his body stiffened and her insides were flooded with his juices. He lay on her, idly fingering her hair, lost in his pleasure while she bore his weight with fortitude.

She moved slightly, complaining, and he pulled out of her. His cock was still semi-erect and covered with his residue. Her finger stole to her cunt, now well-irrigated and smooth to the touch. With some application, her own pleasure might come. Itagaki ignored her, staring intently at his groin. She looked too, imagining it coming into her again, but softer this time, and good. She sat up and played with her entrance, her fingers in the warm ooze. He looked at her face then followed her gaze to his prick.

"Clean me!" he said roughly.

"What?" she smiled roguishly. Perhaps he was ready for some real love after all. Itagaki was a strange and remote man. His words penetrated and she started to get up for a bowl of water and a washcloth. It occurred to her that this was a very bourgeois thing to do, the service a wife would supply her husband.

"Not that way." His harsh words broke into her musings. "Stay where you are!" He rose to his knees before her, then guided his partial erection to her mouth. She looked on in horror. "Clean it!" He shoved his hips forward and the smelly, sticky pole was thrust between her lips. Unwilling but unable to protest, she sucked the cock in. She licked the underside and he twitched inside her mouth. He pulled out and she began licking and cleaning the entire length of the shaft. She carefully licked and sucked at the last drops of juice that hid under the head. He grunted with satisfaction. She moved backwards, exposing the length of the retumescent shaft, now clean of every drop of salty juice. She found herself enjoying the salty cheesy taste. Suddenly his cock jerked with impatience. She hurriedly sucked at it again as he surged forward. It jerked again against her tongue, and then her mouth flooded with fresh come.

Itagaki removed himself without a word and zipped up his jeans. "Haven't finished with the copying yet? Get on with it!" he said gruffly and turned to other business.

She dressed and wandered out to the campus. For once the large-character slogans, glaring red on all the walls failed to excite her. She was tired of all the political activity, and wondered what it would be like, once, to have a man who was interested in her, not her political ideas. Even if he liked her body for its own sake, nothing more. She saw the brightly dressed female students in their sneakers and imperialist-sloganed sweatshirts, and fell into a daydream: herself as a bourgeoise, married, serving tea and cakes to her husband as he came home from the office.

Her musings brought her into an area of the campus she did not usually enter. For good reason, she remembered, as she saw several students were performing a strange dance on the paved way. Bright red strips of cloth rose and descended, curved gracefully through the air. Sickened, she turned away. It was no dance, and the red ribbons were tied to the iron bars with which the gang were disciplining one of their number.

She recognized them as members of the Radical Pro-Worker Left Faction: her group's arch enemies. One of their number, a pale, bearded youth she remembered from rallies, had apparently erred and was now suffering the penalty.

She turned rapidly and walked quickly away. The movement attracted the attention of two of the Faction's lookouts. One of them recognized her and they followed. Heart pounding, she rounded a corner and walked through an arch. There was a doorway there, but she knew it led through a long corridor to another exit: Right before the squad that was beating their Faction mate.

A young man engrossed in a book was leaning against the door. He saw the wild look on her face. His expression was quizzical, but also seemed kind. Hanako ran up to him.

"Can you help me? Please, they are following," she babbled. She had used metal pipes herself, but now that she was the object of attention, she trembled in fear.

Andy slipped off his tie. He quickly tied her hair up in a ponytail to alter her looks. Then he took her by the shoulder and turned her around, turning his back to the archway. She was now facing the arch. He put his arms around her, tilted her head back and pressed his lips to hers. There were hurried steps behind him. Andy looked casually over his shoulder.

"Hey, can't a fellow get some privacy around here without kooks peering on?" he asked in English. Then added in broken American accented Japanese "Hey, go away, we're busy."

The two Radical Faction toughs gave him barely a glance, grinned awkwardly at the *gaijin* and raced off into the building in search of their Communal Faction rival.

Andy released her and stepped back, looking her over. She was rather dirty and unkempt, though beneath was an elfin beauty. Dressed in a rather grimy sweatshirt and jeans, her feet wore rubber thongs and her toenails had dark crescents under them. She was still shaking with fear and her dark eyes jerked about.

"What's the problem?" Andy asked softly.

"You are American?" she said suddenly.

"Yes," he said in unaccented Japanese.

"Student?"

"Sort of," he answered patiently.

"You stay in student dormitory?"

"Not that much of a student," Andy laughed. She noticed his nice white teeth.

"Can we go your apartment?" she asked in broken English. "I must get away. I must have place to stay. Tonight I stay with you."

In her anxiety, she struggled with mangled English, not noticing he spoke perfect Japanese. "You can fucku me if you like." Her eyes still peered at the entrance to her right and at the pedestrian walkway beyond the arch.

He shrugged. Not before you've had a bath, my beauty, he thought.

Hanako came out of the bath wearing his shirt. It clung to her damp body. Her hair was wrapped in a towel. She had even made some attempt to clean beneath her nails. She slipped into bed beside him, spread her legs and reached for him. "Come, make love to me now, I want to go to sleep."

He stared at her. "Is *that* what you expect?" he asked.

"OK," she nodded indifferently. "I will do it."

Hanako pushed the sheets aside and bent over his flaccid cock. She jerked it roughly several times in her small fist, then sucked the swelling member into her mouth. Andy leaned back, piled up the two pillows, put his hands behind his head and watched as she set to work. His cock, responding to the warm though rough stimulation rose in her mouth.

The door announced Jim's return. "Hey Andy I think I've

got another piece," he called out as he was shedding his shoes. He stuck his head into Andy's room.

"So have I," said his partner. He patted Hanako's head and grinned. She screwed her eyes around and nodded a greeting.

"Looks nice and friendly," Jim said. He waved and went off to have a bath.

Andy started to move into her mouth. She accepted that passively, as if it were no concern of hers. Her mouth merely sucked at his shaft each time he withdrew. Andy felt his climax grow and he pulled out, not wanting to come too soon.

"Lick my balls," he said.

Obediently Hanako lowered her head and lapped at the hairy bag under his penis. She did a workmanlike job, starting on one soft round nut and going on to the other. It annoyed Andy to see her so uninvolved.

"Don't you enjoy sex?" he challenged her.

She shrugged, and her small breasts hanging between her arms jiggled. "Sure," she said indifferently.

"What about girls?"

"If you like."

Andy fell back on the pillow and dragged her up to him. With her face a few inches from his, he asked "Isn't there something you won't do?"

She considered a moment. "Make it with a corpse?"

"You don't care, do you?" He was truly puzzled. He had never had a completely indifferent woman before. "You mean if I wanted to beat you or fuck your ass you'd just lie there?"

She nodded "In the commune we do our best to please other commune members. It is required, you see. I am asked for many times, and of course, I cannot refuse. It would make me corrected." She shivered slightly at the word.

"Corrected?"

She stared back at him.

"What about your own pleasure? What do you like."

"To write," she said promptly, then thinking somehow she had made a *faux pas* she added "To please the commune members, of course."

"Is that why you ran away from them?" he asked, grinning sardonically.

"Those were our ideological enemies," she answered with some heat.

"Well, why come to me then?"

She had no reply. Andy continued. "Tell me what pleases you sexually."

She shrugged. "Whatever you like."

"No!" He insisted. "What do *you* like?"

"Anything," she said. "It does not matter. Only the revolution matters."

"Horseshit," Andy grumbled, and turned her over on her back. He knelt between her legs and poised his cock at her entrance. She was only slightly damp, and he worked the head of his engorged penis back and forth before the opening to her vagina. Gradually, the motions became easier as she became wetter. She closed her eyes and allowed him to explore her with a tentative finger which he added to the head of his prick. He kissed her nipples. They were prominent, dark buds which responded to his gentle sucking motions with tiny erections. He sucked a whole breast into his mouth and was rewarded with a rising motion of her hips. He repeated with the other breast. But except for the involuntary movements of her body, she lay passively beneath him.

He slid both palms under her tight buttocks and raised her slightly. She obliged, not opening her eyes. His cock head nudged the bushy entrance to her slit, then pushed inside. She opened her legs as wide as she could to accommodate him.

Andy slowly fed her the length of his shaft. He stopped when he felt their pubic bones come together, then slowly let his weight down onto her taut belly.

They lay unmoving until Hanako opened her eyes and said "Why are you not moving?"

"I was waiting for you," Andy said. "There's no urgency."

She closed her eyes again but slowly this time. He squeezed her buttocks gently, then began stroking the length of her thighs and lower back. She began to respond and her breathing quickened slightly. Andy started to move inside her, rubbing the length of his shaft against the walls of her channel. When he pulled back, she tightened her legs around his buttocks. "It is good," she murmured, without opening her eyes.

He stayed on her, agitating his cock slightly. Hanako's lips parted and she started breathing more heavily. Andy sucked in one, then the other breast, trying to fill his mouth with as much of her soft flesh as he could manage. Her hand suddenly came around his back and clamped onto the muscles of his ass. She squeezed roughly and her whole body stiffened. She uttered a strangled cry as Andy ground his hips against hers and pulsed hot fluid into her. He panted heavily as he withdrew and rolled off her. She looked at him through half lowered lids.

"Was that good?" he asked her, then cursed. It was one banal question he always tried to avoid.

"Of course," Hanako said, passionless. He stared at the ceiling and they listened to Jim sing as he towelled himself off in his room.

"Go over to my brother and give him some," Andy instructed her. She slipped out of bed without a word and walked over the tatami to Jim's room.

Jim looked up from inspecting his penis, shrunk from the

cold air. He blushed. "What do you want?" he asked her roughly.

"Your brother sent me to you."

"Try her," Andy advised from the other room. "You're in for a surprise."

Jim smiled. "OK. What's your name?"

"Omi Hanako," she said and reached for the hardening male member. He turned to face her and she slipped her lips over the engorging head. As she sucked the cock hardened and swelled inside the warm moist cavern of her mouth. Jim leaned over and nibbled at her back. She did not respond. He pinched her small breasts lightly, then stroked her cheeks and sides. To his surprise she seemed completely engrossed in blowing him and there was no response to his touching her. He stood straight and watched her head bobbing over his prick.

Andy was standing at the door. Their looks crossed.

"Peculiar, isn't she?" Andy said.

"What's with her?" Jim asked. Unconsciously his hips were pushing into her mouth and he fucked himself against her tongue.

She seemed to be treating Jim the same way she had him. Andy's cock unfurled and he shrugged. Why not? They could do whatever they wished with her. The dark patch between her legs was clearly visible as she sucked at Jim on all fours. Andy walked up behind her and stroked the furry mound. She twisted her head and seemed ready to protest, then went on with her work. Andy dug his middle finger to the knuckle into her cleft, searching out the depths of the hole. With his other hand he started pinching and tickling her clitoris. Jim's hand joined him.

"Gotta teach this lady a bit about sex," Jim murmured. "She's been fucked, but I don't think she's been loved."

Andy stroked a muscular bun thoughtfully. "Right you are,

brother." He knelt behind her and began teasing the entrance
to her vagina again, the tip of his stiff prick never actually
entering, just moving lazily over all the surfaces it could
touch. Reflexively, she arched her rear backwards in an
attempt to capture the male rod. Andy avoided her grasp and
continued to push against the lips and clitoris. Hanako felt a
rare rise of pleasure in her groin. In most cases the pleasure
was brief as she pleased one or another of her commune. This
time it went on and on, changing the rhythm and the meaning
of the other cock that she was teasing in her mouth.

"Roll her over," Jim said.

Hanako lay flat on the bed, her arms sprawled and her legs
wide. Jim kissed her, holding her head to his as she sought to
escape. The kiss was long and lingering. His tongue explored
her mouth thoroughly, never staying long, fleeing her own
tongue when she pursued, chasing when she retreated. He
kissed the side of her mouth, then her jaw and neck. She
began to respond, to anticipate and hope for the feel of his
breath on hers.

Andy applied his lips to her pussy. She was familiar with
the sensation, but surprised at the difference. The commune
members who had gone down on her had done it in a spirit of
exploration, pleasant but rough. Andy's mouth was not biting
and straining at her flesh. Instead, his tongue lingered on the
soft places, moved to the channel and dipped deeply into it,
responding to her wishes as she squirmed when he touched
the right spots.

Andy was gratified to note the slim girl's response. Gradually, the tautness left the beautiful tendons that ran from
crotch to thigh. Her belly began to churn against his mouth.
He could taste his own sperm on her lips, but in the concen-
tration of what he was doing, was unconcerned. Her movements grew faster and one of her hands tangled in his brown
hair, urging him away, then on, then guiding him to the

deepest places of her pleasure. He screwed up his eyes and noted that Jim was sucking at her breasts. She held them up for him with one hand as her head bobbed from side to side. Finally, Andy felt the first of a series of explosions as the muscles of her lower torso contracted. He lapped harder and faster at her clitoris, and heard the moan that grew deep in her throat.

Jim licked his way up her chest again, pausing at the angle of her jaw, at her ear, then returning to possess her mouth. She eagerly sought him this time. Her tongue flicked against his just as her cunt clenched in a violent orgasm which repeated in a long, diminishing series of waves. Slowly, she came down. The mouth that had incited her below gradually made its way up her body to one breast. The other mouth tickled down to the other mound and both sucked at her hungrily. She cradled both heads in her arms, her eyes full of life. Hanako raised herself slightly and looked at the two faces. They were so similar, yet so unlike, like twins photographed in negative and positive.

"I want to please you, too," she pleaded.

Obligingly the two men rolled over on their backs side by side. Hanako straddled Jim, then leaned over and engulfed Andy's cock in her mouth. She laved the length of the shaft, reaching the balls as she descended slowly the length of Jim's erection. They supported her and the speed of her movements increased. Before Jim could begin to come, she rose off him and straddled Andy. Her mouth tasted her own juices on Jim's cock. The men stroked her body, reaching for the deep crevices, fondling the smooth bulges. She felt her own climax rise with that of the two men she was loving. She moved quickly on Andy, forcing his cock deeper into her, encouraging his climax. At the same time she controlled Jim's excitement, stopping to lick the tip, then dipping the length of warm flesh deep into her throat.

Andy began climaxing. He clutched Hanako to him, grinding his hips high in the air. His come spurted out of him, adding to the wetness of her interior. For a brief moment she withdrew from Jim's cock with her mouth and pressed her lips to Andy's. He groaned and subsided and she rose from him and hurriedly stuffed Jim's engorged penis into her. Her ride was brief; the activity so far had brought him no relief. He roared and his body arced off the bed. Hanako clamped her hips to him and her mouth sought his. Now it was the man's head that thrashed from side to side. She felt her own climax just as the last of his semen poured upwards into her, and they subsided together, her sensitive channel hugging the length of his manhood.

Hanako lay between her two lovers. Their hands were idly stroking one another's bodies.

"That was wonderful," she said dreamily. "It is better than revolution . . . . I wish I could have it forever. I am sad it is over."

"You can come again," said Jim in a whisper. He idly thrummed a soft nipple.

"No. I cannot. They will suspect my absence, label me a deviant. Then . . . then there is correction."

"What is 'correction'?" Jim asked.

"I must go back tonight," she said, rising from the bed and taking a last look at the twins. "I cannot stay."

She padded into Andy's room and retrieved her clothes. They followed her and watched her dress silently. She put her hands on their shoulders, hugging them briefly to her. "Till we meet again." For a second she rested her head on both chests, hugging them tightly. Then she was gone.

CHAPTER 11:
Swan Song

Her feet were held in the air, knees to full breasts that quivered with effort despite being spread across her chest. Jim loomed above her. Andy could see Jim's hard penis as it sank between her plump lips. Lynette was completely open. Her tiny ass bud winked at him. Wetting his middle finger, Andy made tiny circles around the opening. She tried to push his hand away, but Jim held her hands down beside her head as he rose to crouch over her and drove his cock into the welcoming vagina like a piston.

Andy thrust his finger into the hole, widening it. The strong muscles resisted the anal penetration and Lynette moved uneasily. He moved it about, the back of his hand coming into contact with Jim's balls. Jim was breathing heavily, and his balls slapped her flesh with wet sounds that matched the panting. Andy inserted a second finger, moving both slowly in time to the panting couple. Finally he lay crosswise to her ass. He guided his heavy prick to the tiny opening. She could see his face by raising her head from the pillow. She shook her head when she felt the head of his cock at her anus. He persisted and the prepared hole widened. Lynette said "No, no," but in rhythm, in time with Jim's plunges. Delicately, trying not to pain her too much, Andy forced his way into her ass. He could feel the Jim in her vaginal canal, and as he inserted himself deeper, the two men began to interfere with each other's movements. Finally Andy found that by raising himself a bit and allowing Jim to do the work they could both feel comfortable within her.

Lynette was gasping and puffing. The invasion of her rear was painful at first, but as she got used to it, a randy sensation pervaded her body. She started squealing uncontrollably. Her mind conjured up images of the two cocks pushing inside her, and wished she had a cock herself to feel the insides of a woman as perfectly as she was being felt.

"Now isn't that better?" Jim asked.

She looked into his face. "You didn't have to force me," she said.

"That's not the way it looked to us."

She had turned up at the apartment without notice. Andy and Jim, both busy, had made it clear that her presence was unwelcome. But she had stayed, chattering away, obviously hoping Andy would take her not-so-subtle hints and leave her with Jim.

"Why don't you just screw Andy?" Jim bluntly asked her.

"What?" she had squeaked. "What do you think I am?"

"A girl who came here to be screwed," he had answered.

"That's not *true*," she said hotly.

"Oh yeah? I bet your cunt is all wet," Andy said. "As I remember, it gets wet very easily."

"How the hell do you know, you shit," she had stormed.

"Because I felt it. And fucked it." They told her about the night she had been there, and she blushed a deep scarlet. Furious, she had picked up a large ashtray, the closest thing at hand and tried to brain Jim who was now laughing. They had restrained her, and the wildly struggling girl had raised the excitement regenerated by their reconstruction of the earlier night. Their efforts to calm her soon turned to undressing her and themselves.

Stuck deep in Lynette, Andy was suddenly conscious of the ringing of the doorbell. It took a few more seconds to remove himself.

Koihara Natsumi stood at the door. She had on the severe business suit she wore to work at the landlord's office, and an expression of slightly sulky compliance. Andy welcomed her.

"Come in, Natsumi. You are just in time."

She closed the door, then bent to unstrap her shoes. Looking up she found herself facing Andy's erect cock.

"Say hello first," he said brightly.

"Andy-san, you mustn't do things like this," she said in the baby-doll voice they both knew brought his blood to a boil.

He nudged her with his cock and she obligingly opened her mouth. The engorged head slid past the lipstick-coated entrance and lay on her tongue. She hollowed her cheeks and sucked at the large head. The taste was one she was learning to like.

"That's very nice, Natsumi," he said as he withdrew. She rose and he kissed her, his tongue probing deeply into her hot mouth, one hand squeezing a flat breast, the other clutching at her rear. She was glad she had removed her foundation garment before coming. She thought she looked fat without it, but if *he* liked it, she was not going to go against his wishes. Andy undid the buttons on her blouse and walking backwards, led her to the bedroom.

She stopped at the entrance as she saw Lynette alone in the bed. The wide-hipped *gaijin* girl had her legs parted. The patch of dark hair at the juncture of her thighs was matted and Natsumi could see her slit, gaping and gooey. A sheen of moisture highlighted her thighs. Jim was nowhere to be seen.

"I didn't know you had company, Middler-san," she said, her voice expressionless. She turned and hurried back to the door. Andy raced after her, grabbed her shoulder and spun her around.

"You wanted to be my steady?" he asked.

She nodded. "I will come another time." Her voice was still flat.

"I said 'you will do whatever I want' and you agreed, didn't you?"

She nodded her head and started to say "But . . ."

He put a palm over her mouth. "You can say 'no' as often as you like, but as long as you want me to be your steady, *you do what I say*, right?"

She stared at him, her thick eyelids turning her eyes to slits.

"Well?" he demanded again. Slowly she nodded.

"Wonderful!" he said. "You may *protest* as much as you want, as long as you *do* what I say, OK?"

She nodded again and he applied his mouth to hers. Her arms slid around his waist and he pulled her head to his, grinding his lips and tongue into her.

"I love the way you speak. I even love your protests. They set me on fire," he murmured in her ear. "Now come and meet both my friends."

"Two?" she said, pulling back.

He pulled gently at her. "Two. We're all going to enjoy you. Remember, talk is OK but . . ."

She nodded and her voice returned to the familiar babydoll tones she used to excite him. "Yes Andy-San. Anything."

It was a promise and they held hands, fingers entwined, as he led her back to the bedroom.

Jim was back in bed, squeezing Lynette's full breasts with both hands. She stared through a fall of dark blonde hair at the Japanese girl.

"You said you wanted to sleep with a real Japanese," Andy said. "Well, here we are."

"Hey, no! Not . . . I'm not a lesbian . . ." She protested.

"Of course not," said Andy soothingly as he moved to undress Natsumi. Lynette stared with fascination as the Japanese girl's golden body was uncovered before her. The two girls studied one another, then Andy led Natsumi to his bed and laid her down, spread her legs, and applied his lips to her waiting cunt. The slim Japanese girl kept her eyes on her rival, stroking Andy's hair possessively.

"Come on Lynette, fuck her," Jim told her with a grin. "We'll hold her open for you."

He and Andy straddled Natsumi's legs and each took one of the Japanese girl's lower lips and pulled it gently aside. The full coral pink of the inner cleft was unveiled to Lynette. She absorbed the strange view for a moment, unsure of how to begin. Andy instructed her by patting her back, and Natsumi smiled at her over her own breasts. Slowly but with growing desire, the blond leaned forward and brought her mouth to Natsumi's pink hole. She hesitated and Natsumi moved impatiently, then her tongue darted forward and she licked at the sour-salty opening. Natsumi shuddered involuntarily and whispered "Go on. Go on!" Lynette complied and applied her mouth fully to Natsumi, licking the two male fingers as well.

She was conscious of one of the men climbing onto her back and spreading her legs. Her eyes were closed and she revelled in the sensation of Natsumi's warm thighs and wet slit. A hard penis probed behind her legs and for a moment she feared he wanted entry into her rear again. But soon the impetuous member found its way into her wet crack and she felt it fill her vaginal channel with thick hard warmth.

She was urged forward until she lay on top of the Japanese girl. The prodding behind her forced her inflamed cunt onto the girl beneath her. Without thinking, she began grinding her mound on Natsumi's soft lips. Natsumi responded by raising her hips and grinding them back. The two mounds meshed and their hairs tangled, producing tweaks of tiny pain from pulled hairs, adding to their pleasure.

A rigid cock appeared before their faces and both girls licked at the turgid member. Shyly at first, then with greater eagerness, they began to tongue and kiss each other, too. Lynette found it strange to enjoy the kisses of another girl, but soon she was so sunk into the demanding other mouth with pleasure that she forgot the male member between them.

Lynette feared she would climax before her lover. The demands of the male cock in her vagina were growing urgent. She could hear the slap of the balls against her buttocks as the man's rhythm increased. She opened her eyes to see who was having her, but her gaze was riveted by the look of trust and love that shone from Natsumi's ivory mask below her. There was an obvious tick at the corner of an almond eye and Natsumi's arms clutched Lynette convulsively. Lynette smiled and allowed her own orgasm to flood through her, conscious that the Japanese girl beneath her was doing the same.

Jim pulled Andy back. His brother was lying on the two girls with his full weight, his eyes closed and his cock slowly coming out of Lynette. Jim pulled at Andy again, as the two girls renewed their movements, their eyes on one another. Reluctantly, Andy climbed off and rolled to one side as Jim took his place. Lynette's cunt was relaxed and his cock felt loose. He pushed it in as far as he could, enjoying the sensation. Starting to move in her, he saw Natsumi's eyes open. He shifted and lowered his aim with his hands. The Japanese girl was tight and fresh. It felt distinctly different to that of the girl on top. He pushed in as far as he could, though the entry was hampered by Lynette's full buttocks. He jigged his rump for a few strokes, then changed back to Lynette. The girls' tempo increased and he found it difficult to hit the moving holes. The two girls seemed to ignore him, though Natsumi looked at him occasionally.

Andy was puzzled by Jim's difficulties and contortions until the answer dawned on him. He peered at the juncture of the three pairs of legs, then held his brother's strong cock and guided it into the available holes alternately. The sperm was soon pulsing rapidly out of the thick tube. Jim grunted with pleasure as he rammed himself into one of the cunts, then pulled out and sprayed both bushes indiscriminately with his come.

The two men lay on either side of the women as they watched Natsumi and Lynette explore one another. The two girls sixty-nined with Natsumi on top, then rolled over to lie side by side. Their heads pillowed on each other's thighs, tiny tremors ran through their exhausted, sweat-slicked bodies. Jim, playing idly with his cock, found himself rising again.

The girls scissored their legs together. In this position their cunt lips could rub together with an otherwise impossible intimacy. Jim pulled Natsumi back, knelt over her face and tilted her head back, then inserted his cock into her mouth. She struggled slightly as the tip of his cock reached her glottis, and he relented, pulling back but continuing to fuck her mouth. She sucked hungrily. Andy imitated his brother with Lynette. The massed bush of hair at the girl-juncture writhed and shook as Lynette and Natsumi slicked their cunt lips and clitorises together. The two men peered down at the sight, stroking the sides of their girls and probing with their fingers at the joined pussies.

The flood of Jim's semen in her mouth made Natsumi gag reflexively. There was not much of it, however, and she managed to swallow. Jim rolled off her, and she pulled herself up. Andy was lying to one side, his chest rising and falling silently. Natsumi smiled at him, then pulled the other girl up and their lips joined. Locked in the embrace of another orgasm, they exchanged the flavors of their respective partners.

They drank the warm tea Natsumi had prepared.

"It was very good," Natsumi remarked casually. "Perhaps the best."

"I bet you have a lot to compare with," Lynette said.

"Oh yes," Natsumi smiled. "Many, many."

"You have all the men in your office yet?" asked Jim.

"And all the sailors in the port," laughed Andy, reaching for a bare breast.

"No . . ." she giggled, fending him off. "Only one sailor, really Andy-san."

"Teach you a lot?" Lynette asked with curiosity.

Natsumi hid her mouth with her hand and giggled again. "He was *former* sailor. Now director of company where I work. He is very nice man. A bit old, but *very* good." She giggled again, leaving no mistake about her meaning.

"*I* wouldn't have an old man." Lynette made a face.

"Then you are missing a lot. He is very good. Like Andy-san, only more experience . . ."

Andy reached for her again and she evaded his grasp.

"How like Andy?" Jim asked.

"Oh, he look like Andy-san. Maybe he is a relative, no? Andy-san, do you have a relative in Japan? Leonard Fine is his name. He call himself ah . . . 'Seaman first Leonard Fine, sir.' Then he jump into bed." She giggled again.

"No number?" asked Andy. "Sailors always have numbers."

"Of course, but I do not remember."

"When did you see him last?"

"Two years ago. Aha, Andy-san, you are jealous!" Her eyes opened wide at the thought. "You don't have to be jealous. Now that I am your steady I do not go with him. Besides, he is important director and I have not seen him in

Tokyo for some time. Anyway," she patted Andy's arm. "He is old. He was sailor in Korean War, and maybe he went back to America now."

Andy nodded and sipped his tea. Only Jim noted the tick at the corner of his brother's jaw.

CHAPTER 12:
The captain's sword

Captain C.C. McLane, Sissy to friends and some rivals, examined the room in disgust. The 'Forces hotel in downtown Tokyo was a piece of America she could well do without. The color television and oversoft double-bed kept reminding her of other R&Rs elsewhere around the globe, none of which were particularly satisfactory. And she was horny. She could of course simply cruise the hotel bar, pick out a likely stud and hope that rank was not offended if he turned out to be an enlisted man. But she found many of her compatriots to be uncontrollable gossips. At this stage of her career, that was to be avoided. She stripped slowly, admiring herself in the mirror. Well-formed muscles covered by tawny dark skin. Her pubic hair clustered in peppercorn ringlets at the base of a slightly curving stomach and the faint indication of approaching middle-age. Her face, unremarkable with a broad nose and rather thick lips, had eyes that could shift from softly enticing to absolute command.

She ran her hands over her body, pinching the insides of her thighs, then squeezing her breasts. The black nipples engorged and she squeezed again harder, as her other hand moved to the rapidly moistening opening of her cunt. She slipped a finger between the inner lips, which she privately considered too large and ugly, and diddled her clitoris. She knew as she did so that it would not be enough. She needed a man, but *her* kind of man. With increasing roughness and urgency she moulded and squeezed her own body.

She did not hear the soft knock. She was unprepared when the pink-uniformed maid entered the room, and for a moment they both froze. The maid averted her eyes from the masturbating black woman standing before the mirror, and muttered "*Gomen nasai.*" She turned to go, the fresh towels Sissy had ordered half an hour before still in her hand.

"*Matte!*" Sissy had found her voice and recalled what little she knew of Japanese. Then, in a softer tone, "Come in. Close the door please." Rather than being disturbed by the encounter, she found herself relieved.

They looked at one another. The maid was dressed in the usual uniform of the 'Forces hotel: a too-short pink dress, stockings, and a white apron. Her hair was drawn back, framing a plain face with heavy eyelids. She watched as the black woman, taller than her, full breasts bobbing, walked to the bedside.

Sissy came to a decision. She knew from bull sessions she joined in that the maids at the hotel were available, for a price. And the maid, she hoped, would be discreet. In any case, the maid already had material for plenty of talk, were she so inclined. Sissy groped in her wallet. The direct approach was best. She walked over to the Japanese girl, extended two hundred dollars with one hand, and took the girl's crotch under her dress with the other.

The maid smiled and closed her eyes, only groping with one hand to lock the door. Sissy stripped her quickly and pushed her down on the bed. Without a word she straddled the maid's face and forced her hungry cunt down on the waiting lips and tongue. As the face under her began tonguing and licking, she moved herself violently back and forth. She drew the girl's hands up until they found her breasts and squeezed hard. The girl responded by clutching at the dark tumescent handfuls and milking them roughly. Not content with that, Sissy leaned forward and began lustfully eating the girl with her lips, tongue, and teeth. The Japanese maid responded by arching her back and biting harder at Sissy's drenched clitoris and lower lips. Finally the maid let down a shower of salty-sour-sweet juice as Sissy bucked urgently over her moist face.

"I come again, later?" asked the maid at the door.

Sissy nodded her head. This had been her first lesbian experience, and she was still amazed at her actions. She was not sure she would repeat the performance. Paradoxically, she found herself hornier than before.

The bar was dark and anonymous. She had walked up the slope from Akasaka Mitsuke, away from the centers where foreigners, residents and tourists alike congregated. Finally, in one of the tumble of streets near Aoyama that led off a shopping area, she found a small bar. There was barely enough room for the tiny counter and four stools. The barman, heavy and burly, was talking about sumo wrestling with a tall young Japanese man. Sissy looked at him casually as she ordered a whiskey. The Nikka was harsher than she liked; she followed it with a beer. She gulped it down too and ordered another. The barman took no notice as he filled her order and returned to his talk with the other customer. Sissy watched the television screen. A brainless Japanese pop show was on, something she didn't follow at the best of times. At least the colors were pretty.

"Excuse me?"

She looked up. The handsome young Japanese was looking down at her. "Yes?" She made an effort to sound polite.

He grinned. "I'm sorry, but Sonoda-san is worried. He says it looks like you're intent on becoming drunk, and while he generally has no objection, he's never had a drunk *gaijin* in here before . . ."

"So?" Sissy was belligerent. "I can hold my liquor."

"No, no," the young man said hastily. "It's all right. I'm sure you can. Its just that I needed to reassure him. He rather looks on me as foreigner-in-chief."

"California, or at least the West Coast?"

"Accent gives me away every time," he grinned.

"Sit down," she said.

"Sure. Sonoda-san, this *gaijin* is all right. Not drunk, only lonely," he said in Japanese.

"I guess I am," she said. "You collect strays or something?"

"No, just trying to see if you know any Japanese."

"Sneaky," she said.

"I apologize. Thank you." The barkeep placed two tiny bowls of some purple stuff before them. "Try it?"

"What is it?" Each bowl was filled with a mass of dark tubelike things in a brownish-purple sauce.

"Sonoda-san's apology. Preserved octopus," he said, picking up a pair of chopsticks and separating them. "Try it. Good with drinking."

She made a face, closed her eyes, and took a mouthful. Chewy and salty. Nice flavor if one ignored the horrible tactile sensation. She opened her eyes. The barman placed a small ceramic bottle and two tiny sake cups before them. The young man poured and held the cup out to her. "Drink," he said.

She sipped at the hot liquid. It ran smoothly down her throat, complementing the taste of the octopus. She tried again. Better still. "What's your name?"

"Jim Suzuki," he said. "From California."

"Sissy." They shook hands.

Half an hour later, filled with delicacies she had never tried before and slightly afloat on a sea of warm sake, they strolled through the street. Plastic flowers in the colors of autumn hung in bunches from the lamp posts. Housewives, busy at their evening shopping, passed by. The shops were filled with luxuries that Japanese now took for granted as their parents had not. Jim paused at the entrance to a four-story apartment building. "I live here. Want to come up?"

She smiled and took his elbow. The fire banked in her belly blew up afresh. She looked down at the contrast between her skin and his. "I'd like that."

"My roommate is out for a while. He'll be back later," he said as they entered the apartment. Without another word, sensing her need, he slipped an arm around her waist and drew her to him. Feeling her pull away in reaction, the pressure of his hands increased and he forced them face to face. They looked into each other's eyes for a moment, and then, understanding reached, she struggled silently in his arms. His grip tightened and he ran a hand over her full buttocks while trying to trip her to the ground. Sissy refrained from using the unarmed combat drills she knew. His mouth dropped onto hers and he forced his tongue deep into her. Then he licked her lips, nose and eyes. Finally, they fell heavily onto the floor of the carpeted hallway.

He was on her immediately. His weight spread her legs and he tore at her panties which ripped at the crotch. His hot member probed the scratchy curls of her pussy. Then he lunged into her melting, boiling interior. Sissy sighed with relief and pleasure.

He ripped at her clothing as his hips pumped forcefully into her moist pink vagina. She helped him, unconcerned about her clothes and eager to surrender to him. At last they were naked. Her hands roved over his back as his passed between her buttocks. A finger poked at her anus, worming its way into the muscular interior.

Sissy came, squealing softly as he bit her neck. She was glad to find him still pumping away into her. They rolled over.

She sat above him, riding his brown prick up and down while he roughly squeezed her turgid breasts. "I'm sorry about the . . . No, I'm not," he said. "I saw you at the bar and knew I wouldn't be able to restrain myself. Damn, that was good." Jim kissed her deeply and his hips jerked into her with renewed force.

"Softly now, lover," she cautioned him. The first wild flare was over and having burned off her initial hunger, she wanted to take it more slowly. In response he clasped her to him, mashing her breasts against his chest. Andy, who had just opened the door, gazed at the sight before him with admiration. Aware of the intrusion, Jim spread the girls dark ass and made an inviting motion. Without wasting a moment Andy stripped off his clothes and reached for the cigar tube in his jacket pocket. He spread her buns and slid the lubricated tube up the puckered little hole.

Sissy was not aware the party had grown even when she felt the slick thin tube at her anus. It was a new sensation and she stuck her ass higher in the air to enjoy it, knowing what Jim had in mind. In the past she had rejected such advances, but here and now. . . . The tube slid deliciously up and down past her sphincter, but just as she was beginning to enjoy the new sensation, the tube was withdrawn. She tried to raise herself off Jim's engorged prick, expecting him to shift his aim. Instead he clasped her tightly, forcing her down on him. It was only when another pair of hands joined Jim's and a long tongue licked the length of her crack, moistening the back entry that she realized there was another. She turned her head to see Andy as he squatted behind her and presented his massive cock at her rear entrance.

At first the penetration hurt, but thanks to the earlier insertion and to her own lust, Sissy was able to feel the gradual entrance of Andy's cock into her anal canal. He slid forward until the rough hairs of his pubis were grinding against her full ass. She could feel both pricks inside her, separated by a thin layer of sensitive flesh. Both men pumped slowly into her from either side, while their hands moved about her body and their mouths gently licked her skin.

She came to a climax she had never reached before, mouthing curses and endearments as both men relentlessly probed her. The men stiffened as one, and she felt her insides flooded with semen as they drove deep into her. They collapsed together and rolled over onto their sides, Sissy still held between them. Reluctant to let them go, Sissy squeezed the muscles of both holes. Snuggled up to her, they responded as she wished. Their cocks remained stiff and ready, and before long they were playing a version of ping-pong, and Sissy was again moaning incoherently as their hands rubbed against her exposed flank and breast. She started gasping again, her hands clutching their bodies, grabbing hunks of male flesh and bruising their paler skins. She felt the two shafts rub against one another, separated by scant flesh. She erupted and squeezed both organs as hard as she could, and was rewarded with two mighty thrusts that were followed by the pumping of sperm into both cavities.

Sissy held both pricks in her hand, kissing each one alternately. "You know, you boys look remarkably alike."

"We're brothers," said Jim. "Twins, we think."

She grinned and pulled sharply at the two rods that were filling up again slowly. "Pull the other one. But, *I'm* gonna do the pulling."

"Seriously," Andy repeated. "We are brothers."

The two told her their story, and her face changed from smiling incredulity to seriousness.

"It is kind of strange, particularly since there *is* some sort of connection: Someone is paying our tuition. And we're not sure, but someone is trying to stop us from finding out any more. There have been several incidents." They told her about Sato, about the shadowy Mr. Kitamura and the attack on Jim in Kabukicho.

"We think that Leonard Fine is one of our fathers. It's too much of a coincidence: physical features are supposedly similar, and his association with Daisan and *their* fooling with us." Jim shook his head. "Damned if I know what's going on."

"I wonder, too," she said thoughtfully. "You know, there is a way to trace at least one of those two bozos."

The two male heads leaned towards her. "How?" they said in unison.

"The good old US of A Veteran's Administration. If Leonard Fine served in the US Navy in the fifties, guess where he was going?"

"Vietnam!" said Jim. "Of course!"

"You idiot," she said, tugging at his soft cock. Then noticing what she had in her hands, she started stroking the insulted member again. "No. Korea. Anyway, let me try to find out, OK?"

"How could you?" asked Jim curiously. "The VA doesn't give information to just anyone."

"No big deal," she said. Her white teeth shone in a grin. "I forgot to tell you I'm *Captain* Sissy, US Army."

She lay back on the bed, beautiful and dark against the sheets. "Come on you two, enough goldbricking. I'm going to take you both on, again. I want another sandwich, only this time you'll change places."

Jim tried to roll over on her and she pushed him down.

"No, stay where you are. I want to try something else." His cock was semi-erect, and she helped it along to proper stiffness. She examined him thoroughly, taking her time as she diddled him. Finally she straddled the supine man, facing his feet. Jim raised his head and watched the full dark buttocks descend to meet the tip of his cock. She squatted there, a dark goddess, affording him a full view of her posterior. As she played with his cock on her dark anal button, Andy moved forward and knelt between their legs. He kissed her lips, then drew back. Sissy smiled, raised her dark tits and kissed them, sucking in first one, then the other nipple while squeezing the full bags in her palms. Sissy posed for a moment, the nose of Jim's cock nuzzling her tiny hole, then sank down upon it. She leaned forward and Jim tickled the muscles that surrounded the shaft of his cock as it emerged from her ass. She flashed a single brilliant smile at Jim over her shoulder, then leaned back slowly, impaling herself still deeper on his cock, and spread her knees.

Andy needed no urging. The dark lips of her cunt were spotted with a curly fuzz that had been rubbed into large peppercorn curls. She stroked it, parting the lips and exposing the lush carmine interior. Andy lurched forward and buried himself in the waiting slit. Their mouths met and locked and at the same time she could feel the warmth of Jim's lips as he nuzzled at her ear.

It took much longer this time. They moved slowly to a joint rhythm in which the urgency of orgasm was kept at bay. Sissy noticed Jim breathing heavily, and carefully manipulated them so that they rolled over on the bed, until Andy was on the bottom. This time it was Jim who worked at her asshole, trying to match his thrusts to his brother's. They came, all three of them together in a spattering of joy that left them all breathless. Jim pushed them sideways and they lay locked together, their legs entwined in a multi-colored knot.

Sissy disengaged from the men and they watched her perfect shape as she swayed to the bathroom. She rose from the john and and stepped into the shower. Four strong hands took over. They washed her with their hands and later with a rough washcloth that brought a tingle to her skin and left it shining darkly in the water. Soapy fingers probed her interior and she surrendered to them. They rinsed themselves and her off.

"How about a bath?" one of the men asked, looking at her with renewed hunger.

She laughed and tweaked a soft penis. "Next time," she promised.

"I wish I could take you boys again," she confessed as she dressed, looking at Andy and Jim, sprawled on the bed.

Andy laughed. "I doubt we'd do you much good right now. Except perhaps with mouths and hands. Shall we?"

She shook her head. "Not now. I gotta go. I'll be back though, you can count on it. I'll also look up good old Lenny Fine, your putative dad. He must have been *something,* judging by his kids."

"Sissy?" said Andy tentatively. "Do me a favor though? Next time wear your uniform."

Sissy looked at him speculatively, then nodded.

"I've always wanted to fuck a soldier," Andy grinned.

"An officer," Jim corrected. "Always wanted to screw an officer as badly as they used to screw me."

She sketched a salute in the air and left.

CHAPTER 13:
The full blooms of May

Jim walked into the giant hotel on impulse. The New Otani's prices were such that he could rarely afford them. This time, however, he was flush with the proceeds of a small consulting job. Formally, he was debarred from taking on work in Japan, but in the normal run of things some offers came his way. The hell with the immigration authorities.

The French restaurant in the New Otani was one of his favorites, and he headed for it, down the miles of carpeted hallways that made the hotel into a replica of everywhere and nowhere. He sat sipping his drink, enjoying the hotel's formal Japanese garden.

Lifting his eyes he saw the woman pause at the entrance to the room. He looked in appreciation as she walked across the dining room to a seat not far from his. She had the fullness of maturity. He saw smooth, shapely legs leading up to full haunches which moved pleasingly under the expensive fabric of her dress. Wide shoulders supported a large bust. Her face, too, was round, though it bore a petulant, rather glazed look he did not care for. She brushed short dark-blonde hair from her eyes and looked for the menu. She ordered a drink, and fumed as the waiter misunderstood her Midwestern accent.

"The lady would like a neat rum," Jim intervened when it appeared obvious that the Japanese and Midwestern brands of English were incompatible. She flashed him a grateful smile which transformed her face as it showed a faint dusting of freckles across her nose and cheekbones.

"Thank a lot, I really can't make myself understood. "You're an American?"

"Yes," he said, and smiled, returning to his drink.

She looked in his direction a couple of times. Then, after an internal battle, she rose and stepped across to Jim's table. "Are you by yourself here? I'm Mrs. McCormick. My husband is away, would you like to join me?"

Jim accepted. He was not really in the mood for company, but lonely fellow Americans had an appeal he could rarely resist.

"What are you doing here?" she asked with curiosity as they waited for their orders.

"Computers, and you?"

"Waiting for my husband. He's a businessman, doing something in Osaka. He's in cosmetics. He thinks visiting Japan is good for me. Strange cultures, that sort of thing." She made a face. It was obviously *not* her sort of thing.

She was lonely and bored and thought nothing of saying so. Jim listened sympathetically with half an ear. He enjoyed looked at her, but not hearing her talk. Nonetheless, he couldn't help feel a twinge of sympathy: some people simply could not understand the Japanese, and could not enjoy the country. Even for him, Japanese-looking as he was, the Japanese way of doing things often set him on edge. He nodded occasionally in understanding of her anxiety.

Before long she was May and he Jim; some time later they were riding the elevator up to her floor.

She opened the door and motioned him in. The New Otani suites were not cheap. May was obviously loaded.

"Mix me a drink," she said. Her heels clicked as she reached the entrance to the bathroom. The transition from the silence of the deep-piled carpet to tiles was deafening. High up in the futuristic tower of the hotel, Jim could see west past the towers of Shinjuku. Below him the hotel's Japanese garden spread elegantly, beginning to turn green with the spring. He poured two large rums, neat, then added hot water and sugar from the thermos.

"What did you make?" May asked.

"Hot toddy. No lime I'm afraid."

"How very nice: conventional and unconventional. Most men would have made a cocktail or something, and none would have apologized for *me* not having limes." She laughed and sat on the sofa. Jim moved closer.

"God, how I hate these Japs. Sorry, I didn't mean it that way. I just can't stand this country. Anyway I think of you as an American. Henry just insists on me coming with him, and then he's off to Osaka for business and all I've got to do is stay here and look at temples and eat rice."

"You know that's not really true." Jim was fond of Japan and could rarely stomach carping foreigners, Americans or not, but May seemed like a pleasant afternoon's diversion. "There are things to do . . ."

"Yes." She waved an arm. "I guess so, but the country depresses me. I feel so . . . so . . . *constricted*. You know what I mean?"

"Yes," he said. "Many Japanese feel the same way."

"Well I'm not Japanese and I *hate* it." Tears started rolling down her cheeks.

Jim stroked her cheek. "You shouldn't carry on like that, really. Let me make it better for you. . . ."

She turned her tearful eyes, slightly drunk, in his direction.

Her glass was nearly empty, and she had drunk most of the bottle of wine at lunch. Jim kissed her eyes and murmured, "Mustn't cry." They tasted of salt. His mouth descended to hers and their lips joined. She sucked hungrily at his lips. Her tongue probed into his mouth and her hands reached for the zipper of his pants.

"I don't usually," she murmured, her blond curls bobbing, "but I need it so badly. I'm so lonely."

He responded by groping for her full breasts. Her bra was rather stiff and he allowed himself a hard squeeze. She pulled back from him and he stopped.

"No, go on," May encouraged him. She drained her drink and applied her lips to his again. Burning liquor trickled from her mouth into his and he swallowed, sucking her tongue deeper into his mouth. He reached for the buttons on her dress and pushed her bra up, not without difficulty. He pulled back and she, her eyes closed, allowed him his inspection. Her breasts were very large and pale. Another faint dusting of freckles showed above the line cut across each pale breast by the protection of a bathing suit. Her flat, pale pink nipples were surrounded by large aureoles. Though soft, her breasts still jutted. He handled them appreciatively and May reached for his hands, forcing them deeper into the soft pink flesh.

"I like that," she said, opening her eyes. Still looking at him she reached under her skirt and pulled off her underthings.

"Take me like this," she begged, spreading her legs. "Without undressing."

Jim pushed her back onto the sofa and knelt between her knees. She guided his tumescence to her hungry hole and pulled at the stiff member. Jim slid forward into her and she pulled his head wordlessly to her breast. He sucked and bit hungrily while she twisted under him. Her fat thighs gripped his sides and her heels dug into him unmercifully. It was pure animal rutting and neither of them had the time or wish for any refinements. Jim tried to kiss her but May forced his head down to her breasts again. He bit and sucked the full mounds, now flattened somewhat against her chest. She guided his head from one sensitive spot to the other, always returning to one or the other of her nipples, while his cock pistoned in and out of her. She grunted as the orgasm overcame her, but continued rowelling Jim's behind with her heels until he felt his spunk spurt into her depths. She squeezed mightily with her thighs and contracted her pussy until Jim's cock shrank to uselessness inside her.

Jim raised his head finally from her wet breasts and she smiled at him. "Any more like you at home?" she asked.

"Yes, actually," he grinned. "I have a twin brother."

She looked to see if he was joking, then licked her lips thoughtfully. "Ah . . . what's he like?" she asked. Another question hung in the air unsaid.

"Like me, in some ways . . . Different in others. He has the same . . . tastes."

They looked at one another. Jim was not sure enough to suggest what he thought she was hoping for.

"Maybe you'd like to meet him?" he asked.

"I sure would," she said fervently.

"Now?"

She nodded and her hand crept between their bodies.

"I'll call. Maybe he's at home."

He stood before the telephone, his cock still hanging out of his pants. She rose from the couch and stripped him as he dialled. The line was busy and he tried again. May stood back and examined her prize. Well-muscled and smooth-skinned she could not forebear stroking him. He talked into the handset and she knelt before him, taking his soft cock into her mouth.

"Andy? Hi. I'm at the New Otani. Can you join us? Yes. And how. Get here soon. I'll give you the room number."

She pulled back from his semi-erect cock, swallowing the flavor of their juices and told him the room number. "Ask your brother to hurry. I'll pay for the taxi. And the fines for speeding."

Jim gave the instructions to Andy and then turned to May.

"Let's undress you."

"Shouldn't we wait until your brother gets here?"

"Why? I don't see why we can't have some more fun before he gets here." Jim's hand roved over her body, outside her clothes. She was aware that her forty-year old body was no match for the younger girls he was probably used to. She opened her mouth to protest but he sealed it with a kiss, then stood back and began to undress her. She stood still as he examined her, touching her body lightly with inquisitive fingers.

"OK?" she said, awkwardly.

"I love your body," he said sincerely. His words, and his tone surprised her.

"I'm middle-aged, and sagging," she said truthfully.

Jim nodded, but added "And lush and full and ripe with pleasure. With a full, rounded belly and ass and the biggest mound I've seen." His hands inventoried the parts in question. He rubbed himself roughly against her thigh, his erect cock leaving a shiny trail on the white skin. "I'm going to fuck you lady, to hell and gone. I enjoy older women, just as I enjoy vintage wines."

She smiled broadly and put her arms around him. He grabbed handfuls of her flesh and squeezed as she twisted in his arms.

She laid herself down on the wide bed and spread her thick legs. Jim looked at her flesh with desire, meditatively stroking his rod. She licked her lips at the sight of the tall dark young man and his heavy erection. He spread her cunt lips and examined the full red opening and the bush of dark hair that covered it. She obliged him, spreading her legs wider and supporting her buttocks with her hands. He licked the length of her pussy, separating the inner and outer lips with his own. She groaned slightly, then subsided.

"My breasts. My tits. Take them. They're for you," she murmured between kisses, directing his face downwards. Instead he pulled away from her. She understood immediately as he crawled towards her head.

Jim squatted over her face and directed his swollen shaft into the valley between her breasts. She held the two large pale hills together to afford him ingress and he rubbed himself furiously in the soft pink vale. She watched his hairy balls bobbing over her face and occasionally slapping her chin. She played with them, trying to lick the hairy bag as it swung past. She could see the muscles of his rear flex as he pummelled the flesh of her chest. Her nipples were becoming unbearably taut, and despite his unfeeling weight on her, she began panting. One of her hands dropped from her breasts and reached for her hairy mound. She tugged at her excited clitoris until he removed her fingers and applied his silken tongue. She gasped and returned to squeezing his cock between her breasts, massaging them furiously with her hands as he plunged against them with his penis. The root of his manhood began to pulse and he stopped licking her cunt as his pleasure rose from his balls.

"No. No, not yet," May cried and let go of her breasts, grabbing the shaft and squeezing as hard as she could.

"I'm sorry," Jim said, stopping his movements and looking at her over his shoulder. "I'll get in you . . ."

She shook her head as he rose, and turned around to face her, still squatting over her chest.

"I want to *see* you come on my tits," she said. There was a hidden excitement in her tone. May squeezed her breasts together and he started fucking them again. She watched the purple head appear and disappear from between the imprisoning mounds. The sensation was one she had wanted to feel but had never experienced, and it brought her near her own climax. Her hips and bosom jerked simultaneously as the first of a series of pounding waves swept through her body. Her tits were the center of her sensations. They ached and pulsed, sending frantic messages to her unused cunt, creating frantic, lusty images in her imagination of forceful strangers assaulting her breasts with strong, demanding cocks.

Jim, seeing the effect his action on her breasts was having began to pinch the erect nipples, stiff as icing on a cake. She moaned loudly now, urging him on in hoarse whispers. Her eyes rolled in their sockets, returning to sight barely in time as the dark oval hole at the tip of his cock started emitting spurts of milky-white come that glistened on the taught skin of her tits.

Jim panted and collapsed onto her, then rolled off to save her from his weight. She was looking delightedly at the small pool of juice that clumped on her skin. She squeezed her breasts a final time, smearing the little puddle, and he pinched the nipples until the last of the tremors left her frame.

May was minutely examining Jim's inflamed and tired cock when the chimes rang.

"That's Andy," Jim said.

"Just see that it's not the bellboys, lover," she warned him as he walked, naked and unconcerned, to the door. She heard the mutter of greeting, and a short delay, and then another man came into the room. He was a European. Dark brown hair topped an aquiline face. Heavy cheekbones dominated his looks. He was as naked as the other one, with the same greyhound leanness, the same large curl of pubic hair.

May turned to Jim accusingly "You said your twin brother. What do you think I am, something to call your friends in for?" As she said the words she felt them to be absurd: She was after some fun, so what did it matter? But the fact that he had lied to her seemed a petty and unnecessary thing to do. It just showed, a small portion of her mind said, that you couldn't trust those Japs . . .

"But we are, May. Really, we are twins."

"You're Japanese, he's white," she insisted, rising.

"Excuse me. I'm Andy, by the way. Aren't you being more than a bit prejudiced? You look at Jim's eyefolds and darker color and you say 'they're not alike!' I'd think you could see deeper beneath the surface than that. We *are* twins," Andy insisted. "All you have to do is look at us. A woman like you should be able to really *see* us."

She looked from one face to the other, trying to blank out the generalities and concentrate on the details: eyebrows, ears, bone structure. For a moment the two earnest faces wavered before her eyes, fused together, and she saw real twins, twins identical behind the makeup of different colors.

"I'll be damned," she whispered. "It's true. But . . . but you can't be. Brothers, from the same father, maybe. A Japanese and a non-Japanese mother . . ."

"Twins," they insisted in a chorus. "Same mother, different fathers."

"Impossible!"

The two explained the circumstances and some of May's equanimity returned. "Just what did you mean 'a woman like you'?" she said coquettishly.

Andy sat at the foot of the bed and stroked the sole of her foot, while Jim took her other leg. "Why, I merely meant a woman of your experience. A woman of your lush and lusty presence." His head dipped and he kissed her foot. "A woman of your delightfully sexy appearance." He bit the arch, nibbling towards her ankle. May shivered and then felt Jim's hands sliding up her full calf. "A woman of lusty nature," Andy added. She shivered again. The two pairs of almost matched hands and lips slid up her legs. They drew them apart and she subsided onto a high cushion, watching the two naked men make their way up her body, stage by stage. Her knees were terribly sensitive, and they discovered that soon enough, sending her into alternating gales of laughter and shivers as their lips and tongues explored the dimples she was proud of.

They slid themselves higher. Hands advanced, each pair holding onto a full thigh, thighs she was yet ashamed of, firm, but massive. Now loving hands climbed them, followed by lips which seemed eager to nibble every inch of skin. The two pairs of hands reached the juncture of her legs together. One hand of each pair stroked one side of her cunt, the other cupped a large firm buttock. She raised her ass to facilitate their exploration. The hands, in full coordination explored the soft flowing insides of her cunt. She felt fingers test the response of her rectum. For a moment she resisted, then decided to let them have their way. Experienced fingers lingered longingly on the tiny tight rear entrance, penetrated slightly into the relaxed hole, then withdrew, exploring further up the crack between her half-moons.

They stroked and nibbled their way up her flanks, finally reaching her full breasts. Lingering for only a moment, to her intense disappointment, they nibbled onward until she found two pairs of brown eyes staring into her own. The vision was overpowering and she slowly closed her lids. Light butterfly kisses covered her face and eyes. One mouth, then another sucked at her own and tongues explored her waiting and expectant lips. Involuntarily, her hands rose to clasp the two men to her, and she started rubbing her breasts against their muscular chests.

"The lady loves her breasts," murmured one of the men.

"Yes indeed," whispered the other. She waited tensely, eyes still closed as the heads and hands abandoned her. Her whole body trembled over an edge of fear that her fantasies would not be fulfilled. Two demanding mouths applied themselves suddenly to her taut nipples. Two hands clamped on her breasts, then began a thorough journey around and under each mound. Her shivering increased until her whole body trembled. Two hands parted her cunt lips and fingers were inserted, almost as an afterthought, into her waiting cunt. She sighed tremulously, arched her body and her hips and breasts began jerking spasmodically as she climaxed violently, almost dislodging the searching and knowledgeable mouths. Her tremors subsided slowly, and only rose slightly as she felt Andy's muscular figure mount her and his thick cock shove its way, assisted by someone's fingers, into her palpitating cunt. His come spewed into her unnoticed as she dropped off to sleep.

She woke to find a note by her pillow. On it was drawn the astronomical sign for Gemini, with the twins reversed, and a telephone number. She memorized both, then flushed the paper down the toilet. What Harry didn't know . . .

CHAPTER 14:
Education Mamma

The relaxation he felt was not enough to calm Andy down from the high he had been feeling when Jim had called. They got into the cab at the New Otani, and Jim knew something was up from his brother's grin.

"All right, tell me," he said.

"I've got great news."

"You've found Kitamura!?" Jim's excitement was palpable.

"Who? Oh. No, this is more important. I've landed my first real commission. Someone wants me to investigate this company. I gather they intend to raid it. I'm getting a million yen, flat fee for the trace, and also a commission. That's it boy, I'm on track now."

"Japanese company?" Jim tried to hide his disappointment.

"No. European. The Thunderstorm Corporation. I've never heard of them, but what the hell. I spent the morning setting up the details. This guy pops up from nowhere and offers me the deal . . ."

"Andy," Jim said in a low voice, then, when he saw that Andy was too wrapped up in his future, more loudly "Andy!"

"Huh?" his brother turned to him.

"Andy, has it occurred to you that there are too many people popping up lately? Has it occurred to you that 'Thunderstorm' and 'Typhon' are related?"

Andy's jaw dropped. He swallowed. "It never occurred to me," he admitted. "Think its fake?"

"I don't know," admitted Jim. "It may be a coincidence, but I doubt it. Who hired you?"

"A guy called Hozato. He didn't want to give the name of his principal."

Jim turned on him. "And you, you sap, you're so pleased at landing a job you didn't realize he's playing a game with you? There is no such name as 'Hozato,' but I bet if you read the characters differently it would be 'Kitamura'!!"

Japanese ideograms can be read a number of different ways, depending on context. Jim's interpretation was entirely possible, though they would have to see the name written to be sure. "Didn't he give you his calling card?" Jim asked.

"Yeah. It's printed in English. But why would he be so obvious? If it is Kitamura and he *is* trying to turn me off his track, why use such an obvious come-on? The guy knows I can speak Japanese . . ."

"Yeah, but maybe he also knows you're a dumb *gaijin* who can't tell the *on* reading from the alternate *kun* reading."

"Maybe," Andy said thoughtfully, "but I don't think so."

Later in the day Andy put aside the problem only to face another, more immediate and infinitely more troublesome one.

This time, Mrs. Akabane called ahead. The sessions with Sumiko were becoming strenuous and the university exams were just around the corner. He hoped her mother hadn't found out about his teaching methods.

She sat on the cushion, and bowed low. "I thank you very much for working with my daughter. I know how hard it must be for you. I am very grateful."

Andy watched her lips. Her makeup was very pale, accentuating the thinness of her face and the fullness of her wide lips on which she used a bright red lipstick. "Well I am sorry I am not such a good teacher. It is not my profession . . ."

She looked at Andy doubtfully and somewhat fearfully, perhaps afraid he was about to back out from his commitment.

Politely she asked "It is taking much time from your work?"

He shook his head just as politely. "It is not too bad. She is a very good girl, your daughter." The word "good" had several connotations. "She is doing quite well."

"But it must be very difficult for you. I see you rarely go out much? I can see the light here from the street in the evenings, you see," she said ingenuously.

"That's not so bad," Andy said, laughing. "I have much work of my own to do, and little time to do it. Also, I am not very sociable."

"But even so, you must amuse yourself somehow?"

For a moment he was tempted to hint that "amusement" was to be found in the teaching profession as well. "It is not so bad. I can play computer games," he said, making a joke of it. But she persisted.

"I mean, in Japan you must have some fun . . ."

"I enjoy myself well enough." He was somewhat curt. Usually he was courteous with the insatiable Japanese curiosity about his life as a *gaijin*, but he was anxious to get back to his other problem.

She bent her head, as if chastised by his tone, then said in a low voice "Middler-san, I must apologize. My daughter's studies and my selfishness are taking away both your work time and your leisure, pray allow me to make amends." She shifted around on her cushion and bowed to the floor, looking at him sideways.

"No, no, it is nothing." He used the usual formal phrase but the words stuck in his throat. She was not making the usual polite bow. Instead she flipped her dark grey skirt over her back, exposing the smooth creamy expanse of her behind. She had obviously prepared for this, perhaps had even intended it from the start. No Japanese woman would appear formally in public without stockings. Instead of panty hose however, she wore a garter belt, and no panties.

"Please enjoy yourself," she urged him. "I hope this will make up somewhat for your lost leisure time."

Andy was stupefied and gaped at her. Then he licked his lips.

"I see you are not ready yet," she said, raising her head a little from the floor and looking directly at his crotch. "Perhaps I can help." She left her full, lipstick-covered lips open, leaving no doubt as to her meaning.

The daughter and the mother too, he thought. Andy rose to his knees and unzipped his fly. His cock was swelling rapidly, but was still soft. Mrs. Akabane captured it with her mouth and he thrust forward. She sucked, her cheeks hollowing until he could feel the tip of her nose against his pubis. She moved her head back and forth, using her lips and compressing the hardening meat against her palate with her tongue. When the tip nudged her throat she withdrew to allow it room to grow. Andy pulled her impatiently forward. Though he could feel her fighting her own gag reflex, she did not resist. Her smooth forehead butted into his muscular belly as she sucked at his cock while he controlled the movement of her head. He traced the delicate lines of her ears and face, hidden by her mass of hair. His movements grew rougher as a minor climax, barely controlled, erupted from the depths.

Curiosity overcame him and he withdrew and tilted her chin up. Her eyes were open and he stroked her cheek. She obligingly opened her mouth. On the pink tongue lay the smeared drops of his initial orgasm. She opened her mouth wider, expecting him to resume fucking her face, but he shook his head. She bowed down to the floor and he poised behind her back. Her ass was fleshier, but as smooth and beautiful as her daughter's. He spread the cheeks wide. The tiny anus button showed no signs of having been used. He smiled. Below it lay long thin labiae, covered with sparse hair only in the front. He leaned back to see better and parted the lips to examine the coral cleft and the hole leading inwards. He tested the hole and the lips with his finger. She was rapidly growing more moist. He agitated her with a finger, dipping first one, then two, and finally four bunched fingers into her soft hole.

Clutching one ass cheek he urged her back on his fingers, then pushed her off again. She began moving, slowly masturbating herself against his digits. He widened them somewhat to observe the effects. The membranes of her cunt exuded juices and her movements became more rapid. He slipped a thumb into the hole and pushed down, exposing still more of it while his fingers cupped her mons. Her breathing started coming in harsher gasps and the speed of her movements, now only partly controlled by him, increased.

Using his thumb Andy wet the tiny anal bud. She moved uncomfortably at the strange sensation, but did not try to avoid it. He spread her apart wider. Each hand grasped one of her smooth buns firmly. He rose and directed his prick at the sopping opening. "Please help yourself," she murmured brokenly. The head of his cock found the wide hole easily. He shoved and the head disappeared inside. The shaft followed and she moved back to welcome him. She was deep yet tight, and the initial digitizing of her insides had produced an agreeable smoothness. She bent down to the floor, raising her ass and moved herself back and forth. He released her and watched her work on his shaft. Her movements grew faster and her breath came rapidly. Involuntarily his hips jerked forward to meet hers. He stroked the soft buns, ridged now and again with her effort. He wetted his thumb and opened her crack wide. It slipped easily into her rear hole and she quivered. He frigged her lightly while allowing her to set the tempo, then decided to explore her further.

Unbuttoning the silk blouse was no problem. Her nipples were hard against his palms and he used them to pull her against him and grind his heated hips into her rear. She responded with a practiced motion of her own which sensuously stroked in a counter movement to his. She gasped slightly as he stroked her back and belly, then his hands cupped her ass and mound simultaneously. He raised her left leg high and laid it over his shoulder. The position was uncomfortable for her but she did not complain, allowing him complete access to her stretched pussy. She struggled to balance as he rummaged the length of convoluted flesh and hair between her thighs.

Her bush was long and luxuriant, running now with their mutual moistures. He pinched her prominent clitoris while agitating his thumb in her rear hole again. The speed of her motions against his cock increased and she groaned audibly. He could feel the muscles of her vagina contract against his cock and he stabbed deeply into her. To avoid his own climax, he squeezed deliberately at the base of his cock and slapped her ass to make her stop.

Mrs. Akabane turned her head to face Andy. He smiled at her and said "I do not wish to finish yet."

She smiled in understanding, and he pulled out of her and allowed her to lower her leg to the floor. He started to strip and she helped pull off his pants and shirt. Without a word she stood up and slipped out of her blouse and skirt. She left her garter belt and stockings on to tantalize him, but he motioned them off as well.

Andy licked his lips as he looked at her. She was tall and slim, angular yet graceful. Sumiko would not change much as she grew older. Unconsciously Mrs. Akabane shielded her breasts from his gaze, removing her hands and propping up the two mounds when she saw his gaze upon them. She ran her hands over her body, pleased to note that the motion excited him.

Her hands reached her thighs and Andy asked her "Do you masturbate?"

"Of course Middler-san. Would you like me to?"

He nodded.

Her hand dipped into the depths of her slit and began stroking the length of the two lips. Her motions speeded up to a blur as the sensation began reaching her. Her hips arched forward and Andy dipped his head to see better. Her eyes were closing, then snapped open when she saw his face.

"You also want . . . want the other end?" she asked. There was a slight tremor in her voice, notwithstanding her determined expression.

He nodded again, then smiled. "Yes, I must have you every way possible."

Mrs. Akabane nodded. She did not wish him to devote more time than necessary to frivolities, and this was one way of ensuring that he was relaxed and attentive to Sumiko's English lessons. By providing for him she could insure that he would not be busy trying to entertain himself in bars looking for girls, when Sumiko's future lay in the balance. Sumiko *must* pass the entrance exams by any means possible. It was as simple as that. Now Sumiko's English had improved immensely, and in less than a month's time she would be taking the university entrance examinations.

Mrs. Akabane reached for her bag, gracefully kneeling on one leg before him. Unable to restrain himself, Andy stepped forward and stroked the length of her slim body. She allowed him complete freedom, which he used to stroke and squeeze her feet and thighs, asshole and breasts with inquisitive hands and tongue. She found what she had been looking for: A jar of Vaseline.

Andy stopped her from rising with his exploring hands. Her pose, which twisted her body elegantly, delighted him. "Continue," he murmured.

Mrs. Akabane started stroking her pussy again. She insinuated her left hand, fingers dipped in Vaseline, between their bodies and anointed her rear hole. Andy's hands followed hers and he nibbled at her neck while his tactile sense was rewarded with the feel of her fingers in her most intimate areas.

He pushed her forward and knelt behind her. One of her hands was busy with her long furry purse, the other was gently massaging her rear muscles in preparation for his penetration. One, then two fingers stroked the small bud, enlarging and softening it. Andy pulled her hands away. His cock was hard, standing away from his belly and feeling like a bar of iron. He knelt behind her and she placed her hands on the *tatami* to support their combined weight. His cockhead nuzzled the slick entrance and he gripped her hips tightly. The smooth skin and muscles stretched over the bones of her hips.

She relaxed her muscles, but the tiny opening still resented the massive presence he was forcing upon it. The tip of his cockhead slid only gradually into her hole, which he widened slowly with light pushes of his hips. He arched his body back to observe the effect. Finally only the flanges of the head were visible before entry. Mrs. Akabane did not move as Andy held her tightly. Her flesh dimpled around the marks of his fingers. He pulled her steadily towards him while inching himself forward. The crest popped in, then the length of his shaft disappeared up into her. Her breathing was harsh but she did not fight the invasion.

The sensation was better than any he had ever felt. Her

cooperative passivity made the invasion smooth every inch of the way. At last he found himself embedded in her to his balls. He rubbed his crotch hair against her smooth buttocks until the creamy skin reddened. He pulled out, then thrust home again. She braced herself patiently, and he set out to explore her body. This time he lingered on her empty pussy, filling it with his fingers, attempting to excite her to a climax. His own motions in her bottom became uncontrollable. He pulled hard against her, rubbing his crotch against the softness of her buttocks at each stroke. Unable to resist anymore she gave a cry and tensed her anal ring for one moment. The squeeze was too much for Andy. A stream of milky fluid boiled up from his balls and inundated her insides. He panted on her back, eyes closed, bathed in the delight of his coming while his hands absently fondled her clitoris and the entrance to her vagina.

He withdrew from her rear entrance leaving a slimy trail of residue. Holding on to her hip, he tried to masturbate her to a climax. Mrs. Akabane disengaged from his rubbing hand. "It is not necessary Middler-san. It is for you. To provide some relief while you tutor my daughter. Is this enough for you? Would you like me to stay some more?" she asked solicitously. Andy shook his head weakly. He lay on the floor and watched her wipe herself, then dress calmly. As she adjusted her stockings and stood to go she asked "When would you like me to come again? This week? Or perhaps not until next?" It was quite clear that either time would suit her.

"Next week," Andy managed to mutter.

She bowed at the doorway "Thank you for everything you are doing," she said formally.

Ten minutes later he was still staring at the door, stupefied.

CHAPTER 15:
Sissies do fight back

"You don't have to look so surprised," Sissy said. She was wearing full uniform, something few American servicemen cared to do in Tokyo when not on official business. The Japanese were sensitive about uniforms, particularly those of foreign garrisons in their country.

Jim let her in and she shed her issue shoes.

"What are those?" Andy asked admiringly, looking at her badges.

Sissy smiled. It's true, she decided, all the little girls and boys love a uniform. And she was proud of it. Not only of what it represented, but of what it demonstrated about her personally. And the uniform did something to the beholder, she decided, noting the tension in Andy's pants. Thought led to action, and as she cupped his balls in her hand, she crooned, as she knew men in the same uniform would. "Come to Mamma, cutesie. Let's have it now."

Andy was surprised to find himself flat on his back on the tatami, with Sissy's dark face grinning down at him from her full height. She straddled his supine body, raised her skirts slightly and said "Have a good look, lover boy. Now take it off."

165

Andy did not need another invitation. His hand climbed her
nyloned leg to her crotch, grasped a handful of the sheer
fabric, and pulled down. The nylons puddled on his chest and
she stepped out of them. He could see the deep dark snatch at
the junction of her legs. It looked moist, and ready. Keeping
one eye on it, he unzipped his pants and raised his hips from
the floor to free himself. His cock sprung erect and she
squatted down, pulling up her skirts to give herself more
freedom to move.

She rode his cock, inserting it only gradually into her wet
hole. Once he was fully inserted, she leaned forward and
pinned his roving hands to the mat near his head. "I'm going
to fuck you dead, boy," she crooned and began to raise her
bottom and force it down in sharp jerks. He struggled but she
was too strong and knew how to wrestle better than did he.
Her pubic bone mashed down on his and he felt the jar.

Jim stood before her. His hands reached for her hair and he
pulled her forward. Eagerly, she sucked in his long thick
shaft. He retreated to allow her to straighten her throat, then
gradually eased back in until the rough hairs at the root were
tickling her nose. She breathed easily and her tongue laved
the length of the shaft embedded in her throat.

The three of them rocked easily to a climax and her vaginal
and oral canals were both flooded with their sperm. She
clutched Jim's ass to her, to let the engorged muscle subside
naturally, then gradually let it out of her mouth. Andy's cock
plopped from her cunt at the same time. They lay on the
warm *tatami*, undressing her from the legs up.

"Oh," she said. "I have that stuff for you. About your
father."

Jim and Andy stopped tickling her feet and raised their
heads. She reached for her uniform jacket pocket and extracted a flimsy. "Hm, lets see, here we are '. . . Fine, Leonard.
Seaman First. Discharged 1953. Yokosuka, Japan. Served . . .'
this wouldn't interest you. Here we are. No living relatives.

Busted twice. Once for gambling, once for AWOL and entering an Out of Bounds address, also in Yokosuka. Never
claimed any veteran benefits except his severance pay. Says
here 'Officer material,' but there's no indication he ever put
in for officers' school. Picture. Its a fax, not very good, of a
picture taken thirty years ago.''

Andy reached for the paper and Jim studied the picture
over his shoulder. It showed a dark, rather chubby looking
sailor with a large hooked nose. He was smiling vaguely as if
amused at something off camera.

"Thanks Sissy," said Jim. "We don't know what to say."

Andy was too wrought up to speak.

"Don't say, lover boy. Just do!" She reached for them
again. Jim struggled to reach her crotch before she could
reach his, and Andy, as if waking from a dream, joined in.
She giggled loudly, white teeth flashing.

"I have a suggestion for you boys," she said. "Let's play
soldier."

"How's that?" asked Jim.

"Get drunk and roll in the gutter?" said Andy.

"Hell no! You think that's all we do? Come on you
luggards, let me give you a taste of the real thing." She eeled
off the futon and stood up. They stood up, too. She bullied
them into line, took two paces back and looked both nude
figures up and down.

" 'Ten hut," she called out in a voice she rarely needed to
use. They tried to stiffen to attention, but only managed to
look ludicrous.

"I said 'attention' you rubber-dicked nothings," she slapped
each thigh playfully but smartly. Both men shrank from the
blows which were too near their maleness and too hard for
comfort.

"I'll never make soldiers out of you."

"Thank God," Andy shuddered. "If that was a sample,

I'd rather be a civilian. In any case, civilians should order the army around, not the other way . . ."

"Speaking of which," Jim said, lunging for her. The three of them rolled on the rough, slick *tatami*.

"Ohhh, god, that's wonderful," she gasped as Jim's prick entered her cunt. They lay side by side while Andy masturbated in the crack of her ass, nudging the tiny bud of her anus occasionally with his member.

She looked back at Jim and her expression changed instantly. She flung both men from her and leaped to her feet, over them with a scream neither had ever heard before.

The two pinstripe-suited Japanese were as surprised as the twins. Both wore the black shirts, silvery ties, and crew-cuts which were the uniform of the *yakuza,* or Japanese gangsters. They had managed to open the door quietly and slip inside. They had not noticed the trio on the floor until it was too late. The nude black figure flying through the air at them created a greater paralysis than the scream. The first one, less lucky than his companion, received the full power of Sissy's *tobe yoko-geri* flying kick to his solar plexus and fell to the floor. His companion barely had time to deflect Sissy's *gyaku-zuki* fist, and before he could counter, she followed with a sharp blow to his neck with the *shuto* side of her stiffened palm. He managed to block that too, but the small hall did not allow him enough space for a proper stance. Her hand curled at his elegant lapel and pulled forward. He followed, hoping to roll forward and an excruciating pain tore through him from his balls. Sissy lowered her knee and stomped his instep, then threw him to the floor with a hip-twist. She moved back, her eyes narrowed, ready to attack again, and almost backed into Andy and Jim who were hurrying ineffectively to her rescue, one armed with a kitchen knife, the other with a skillet.

"I think they've had enough, boys."

The two intruders staggered to their feet, supporting one

another. Unexpectedly, they bowed painfully. Their eyes glittered and Sissy's muscles tensed. But instead of attacking, they bolted through the open door and retreated down the corridor. Jim was all for following until he noticed they were all still undressed. Andy rushed to the window, in time to see the two men stagger out of the apartment building and head towards Aoyama-dori. As they reached the corner, three figures moved out of a shop and closed on the two. There was a brief exchange, tense and strained, and the entire group walked off, the two intruders surrounded by the newcomers and obviously still in pain.

"What the *hell*," was all Jim could say. He too had seen the end of the drama.

Sissy joined them. "Well boys, if I hadn't believed you before, I do believe you now," she said drily. "Anyone know what's going on?"

Neither could answer her.

CHAPTER 16:
Southern Comfort

Leaving Nobbins Stop had been the first step away "from the kangaroos and the rams" as Phyllis had put it to a friend. Landing in Tokyo had been the second. Not that she had any particular interest in sloping eyes and pagodas, but Tokyo was at least one step closer to the rest of the world than Brisbane. She was standing at Yodobashi station looking lost when Jim saw her for the first time. Yodobashi station is the junction of a number of trains, subway and elevated, so her lost look was not so surprising. After eating lunch at one of his favorite *kabayaki* places, he passed the station again. The dark blonde tourist was still standing there, looking as lost as before. She was attracting plenty of attention too. Her very short shorts had much to do with it. And her mammary endowments were unhampered by a bra.

As he walked past her Jim looked at her again. She was too heavy to wear what she did, with thick thighs and full ass. But she did look lost and terribly confused, so Jim decided to play the Samaritan. He intended no more than showing her the way and moving off.

Her relief was obvious, and after he explained that Yodobashi and Iidabashi were *not* the same place and had been thanked in a heavy Australian accent, he moved to leave. She still looked a bit desperate though, so as she shouldered her bag he impulsively gave her his card.

"If you're really in trouble and need an interpreter, call me," he said generously, not expecting her to do so.

"I'm so grateful, you have no idea." She smiled, and her broad mouth widened. The 'I' sounded like 'oi,' the 'you' like 'yer,' but he understood her. He looked once more, at her full thighs, the tiny curl of dark pubic hair that had escaped from under her shorts, and the full, pink-tipped breasts that swayed under her blouse. Bowing carelessly, he left.

Jim was in the midst of a complicated operation, trying to modify the machine language routine for a computer game on his PC when the bell rang.

"Get it, will you Andy?" he called through the open door to his room.

Andy shuffled to the door, zipping up his jeans. He had been dozing, wondering whether to go out.

"For you," he said laconically, appearing at Jim's door. Silently he mimicked huge breasts. Jim wondered.

"Hi," she said breezily, stepping on the tatami with her shoes. "Remember me? We met at the train station this morning."

"Sure, of course. Do you mind taking off your shoes?"

"Oh, terribly sorry." She removed her shoes while standing on the *tatami* and Jim looked at her with displeasure. He showed her in.

"What can I do for you?" he asked. Andy lounged in the doorway, his torso bare.

"I'd like to stay the night if I may?"

Andy left the apartment to them and went off.

Phyllis allowed Jim to stroke her breasts and kiss his way

down her chest, but she stopped and moved off when he tried anything stronger.

Nevertheless, the one night turned into several. Jim was puzzled by her. She displayed an interest in sex and a freedom of language that put her in a separate class. And she was obviously no virgin. She talked freely and in great detail about her experiences, looking at the two men to see if they appreciated her exploits. Men and boys in Nobbins Stop, where she came from, had apparently benefitted from her charms greatly. Andy tried turning her on several times only to have her decline his advances with a frigid departure from the room.

"I don't understand this chick," he confessed to Jim. "She's a cock-teaser, that's all."

"That doesn't bother me so much," Jim said untruthfully. "What bothers me more is that she's a moocher, an ungrateful one at that. Just look at this room!"

The girl's clothes were scattered about. Her pack, half open, lay on the *tatami* and various items spilled from it to the floor. She helped herself to the food in the house, covering bread and plates with a dark brown, nauseating spread called "Vegamite" which smelled to Andy like a particularly revolting soy sauce.

"She is a pain in the ass," he agreed. "I'd love to get rid of her, short of throwing her out bodily . . . Besides, I want some return on our hospitality. Those fat thighs are getting to me."

"She won't allow you past first base on that one," Jim said heavily.

The more he thought about her, the more Andy's temper wore thin.

"We both ought to . . . Oh no man, you're not thinking . . ."

"There she is, having a shower at our expense, after sleeping in our house, wandering about Tokyo all day. This is like a first-class hotel for her, man. Shit, I'm tired of being used. Let's use her for a change. Three days is more than enough.''

"I've never raped a girl before," said Jim doubtfully. "I've never needed to. It's not . . .''

"I know," said his brother. "But she has been cock-teasing us for three days, and we can either fuck her or throw her out, because I'm going crazy. Besides, we're not exactly new to that, anyway. What about Lynette?''

"That wasn't rape," Jim protested.

"Near enough.''

"She wanted it . . .''

"That's bullshit, and you know it. Rape her because she really wants it. Or rape her and she'll start enjoying it. That's real bullshit. At least be honest. Lynette got turned on, but it was really Natsumi who did the job on her.''

"So what are you saying? We shouldn't screw her?''

"No, hell no. We force her, but let's be honest and say we're forcing her, not that she'll enjoy it. She's a bitch and she's using us, so I don't say we shouldn't use her, willy nilly, but don't get on any moral bullshit you don't believe in. You're a creep and I'm a creep, and let's leave it at that.''

Phyllis stuck her head out of the bathroom. "Andy love, don't you have a dry towel? This one is wet.'' The tip of a generous tit showed over the tiny towel she was holding and the door hid the rest of her body. Jim glared at her and she ignored it. "Come on love, I really need it.''

"That does it. OK brother creep, let's get her. Not because she deserves it: she deserves being tossed out buck naked as she is. But because I want to do it.'' He smiled and rose, saying in a louder voice "Sure Phyllis love, I'll give it to you. It's in the bathroom.'' He stepped toward her.

Bewildered, she looked behind her for the expected closet. Andy's arm went around her waist and he lifted her into the air. She gave a horrified squeal and started to thrash wildly, but by then she was out of the bathroom and Jim was on her as well. She started to scream and Andy clamped one hand over her mouth. Jim hugged her wet legs to his chest with one arm while supporting her weight with the other.

They bore her into Andy's bedroom. Jim straddled her on the bed and held her down while Andy slipped quickly out of his clothes. She tried to shriek and Jim covered her mouth with his hand. Trying to toss him off, she arched her hips off the bed. The bed squeaked in protest as she did when she felt Andy's forefinger probing the damp hairs of her pussy. She bit Jim's palm and when he cursed and removed the injured hand she yelled angrily "You bastards, I'll kill you . . . No, stop, stop." This last was addressed to Andy. Now that he was naked he forced her thighs apart and had rammed a finger into her cunt. She shrieked again and Jim clamped his hands back over her face. Andy slid forward and pressed his knees against her tightly. Jim escaped, but not before she tried to dig her blunt nails into his chest. Both of them wrestled her back down and Andy clamped her arms to her sides with his knees and arms.

He held her shoulders down, pressing with his body, and looked into her face. She shook her head from side to side to avoid his hungry mouth. "Let me be, you bastards, you bloody pommy SOBs. Go away."

Jim pulled her ankles up suddenly and pushed her knees to her magnificent chest. Andy helped him by slipping off her and throwing an arm around her knees, causing her to curve in the grip of his arms. Jim stood back and admired the view. Her full buttocks were open exposing an almost hairless pair of thick outer lips. The brown hair grew in profusion towards her belly, but the lips of her cunt and the little hole of her rear were smooth.

He stripped quickly. His cock was fully erect. He teased

the entrance to her cunt with the tip of his cock for a moment, letting it dip in and out, swirling it around the lips and butting it into the stretched tendons of her thighs. Her angry moans and mutterings were turning to something more demanding when he finally plunged in. She gasped and moaned again, but with pleasure this time, after all.

Jim squatted over her figure, wanting her to feel nothing of him but the length of his shaft that was plunging in and out of her now-juicy hole. Almost immediately he groaned and Andy could see the white sperm froth over the shaft and cover the extended lips of her cunt. Jim pulled out of her and Andy quickly mounted before she could stop him. He pumped into her, uncaring of her own pleasure. Her struggles decreased in acceptance. She tried to salvage some pleasure for herself from the situation. Her eyes were closed and she grunted as Andy's weight came down on her. Annoyed at her sudden passivity, Andy increased the pace, grunting with effort, feeling and pinching at vulnerable parts of her flesh while Jim watched. But force was no longer neccesary. Andy felt his balls bubble to climax and quickly pulled out of her. Her cunt hole sucked impotently at the retreating shaft. She opened her eyes and glared at both men.

"I'll have the police on you!" she snapped, trying to recover her composure.

"It was you who offered yourself, love," Andy reached for her again.

"I didn't mean both of you!" she yelled.

"We're twins. Fuck one, get the other free," said Andy, examining the overflow of her cunt. She tried to close her thick thighs and he held them open with a strong grip on her ankles.

"Turn her over," Andy said. Again she tried to protest but soon found herself held up on all fours. "Just look at this bum," he said. He stroked her full buns, inserting a questioning hand between them, which caused her to shudder, with fear or delight he could not tell. He squeezed her full breasts and licked at her ear. She tried to turn her head away, then reconsidered and rubbed it up against his mouth, mumbling incoherently.

They started to move together. The feel of her full buttocks and thighs against his belly increased Andy's pleasure. Jim was squeezing her breasts roughly and Andy felt her cunt and legs against her faint protests. The sensations were getting to her as well and she bucked under the man, trying to force more of his hated/desired cock into her. Before he reached his own climax she arched her back at him. Her insides contracted, sending her into a trembling raging heap, hating herself for having been betrayed by her own body; something she had sworn would not happen again with any man, not since Brisbane.

There was a light burst from the doorbell. Jim rose to answer. Michiko Teraoka stood there, dressed in a dark-blue trench coat. She smiled at him nervously. He smiled broadly back. "Come in Teraoka-san. You are visiting us about the registration?"

She opened her mouth to deny it. Jim winked and put a palm to her mouth. She smiled conspiratorially and bent to undo her shoes as he closed the door. Unable to resist, he caressed the curve of her ass as she was leaned over. She pushed back at him. He raised her long skirt and examined the moons of her rear, stroking each mound through the fabric. She leaned on the wall patiently, enjoying his manipulation. Jim flipped her skirt up, lowered her underclothes and inserted himself in her. She gasped and moved back against him. He fucked harder, pushing her roughly against the wall. Michiko squeaked in protest and he calmed her by easing up on the violence of his motions. She was overcome with shudders and he felt her legs tense as a wave of pleasure overcame her, then he slid out of her wet channel and smiled.

"Won't you come in?" he whispered.

"Yes," she said shyly. She cocked her head at the sounds from Jim's room, then turned big eyes on him.

Jim smiled. "Come in. I will show you something. Do you remember I have a roommate?"

"Mr. Middler," she said.

"Yes. He is my brother. We were . . . entertaining . . . a guest. Want to see?"

She nodded nervously, and anticipatory gleam filled her broad face.

"Let me help you off with inessentials first," he said, still whispering. She looked at his excited face, the hook-nosed good looks glowing, and nodded. He knelt before her and slipped off her skirt and underthings, then opened her jacket and blouse.

Jim and a girl in police jacket stood at the doorway and looked at the couple on the bed with interest. Andy grinned.

"Have you ever watched anyone make love before?" asked Jim in an undertone.

"No," she whispered back, but her eyes and attention were all on the scene before her. Jim squeezed her behind with affection.

"Want to watch then? We can show you some things . . ."

She licked her lips and nodded. Jim advanced on Phyllis, his erect cock waving damply in front of him. Phyllis was on all fours. He presented the tool to her mouth. Resigned, she sucked the large knob in.

Jim's cock was wet and smelled strangely but Phyllis took no notice. The thick male meat filled her mouth and she sucked at it, even greedily. Andy's cock was churning her cunt and by now she had abandoned herself to the feeling of pleasure. Jim moved his cock in small circles, extruding her cheeks around the knob, pulling out to her lips, then tickling the back of her tongue. After a while she found that she was able to control her gag reflex and actually enjoy the double fuck.

Jim gestured with his head and Andy turned, his hands still resting on Phyllis's full ass. He smiled at the sight of Michiko, who had crept closer to watch the scene. He pulled her closer and whispered "You must be Teraoka Michiko, our *omawari-san*. I am delighted to meet you at last. My brother has told me all about you."

She started to blush, but Andy pulled her down and covered her mouth with his. There was a second of reluctance before her passionate nature took over and she melted into his arms. Their tongues intertwined and his hands searched for her body through her undone clothes. Her tight little cunt was wet, and her tits were firm, nipples erect. He stroked her gently, then opened his eyes. She was staring past him at Phyllis who had begun enjoying herself. Phyllis was backing forcefully onto Andy's horn while on the other side of her Jim shoved his cock deeply into her mouth. Jim bent forward and squeezed her heavy breasts again. This time she responded, pressing them back as hard as she could against his palms.

Andy took Michiko's hands in his and led her palms to his cock. She delicately traced the length of the shaft to its entrance into the pink wet lips surrounded by dark brown hair that were striving to engulf it. Timidly, she poked an exploratory finger into the hole alongside Andy's staff. Phyllis wiggled her behind in response. Michiko's other hand joined the first and she parted the mounds of Phyllis's ass to get a better view. She traced the tiny pink-brown hole of the anus with a finger. Phyllis tried to protest, fearing the worst, and reached behind her to ward off the digits at her rear entrance. Jim grabbed her hands and forced her down. Startled by the reaction Michiko continued to explore the full cunt and the wealth of soft brown hairs in the front. She found the engorged clitoris and rubbed it slowly, feeling Andy's balls at the same time. Just then Andy found her own nubbin and began to massage it vigorously. Michiko parted her legs, then pushed at Phyllis to part hers as well. Jim watched the scene before him as Michiko entwined herself around Andy while her hands were hidden beneath Phyllis's rear.

"D'you still want to complain to the police?" asked Andy as his cock rooted about in her.

She nodded furiously, her mouth still full of Jim's cock. Her eyes were glazing with pleasure despite her vengeful thoughts.

"Why not do it now then?" he asked laughing, and pulled Michiko Teraoka towards them. She was still wearing her powder blue uniform jacket. Andy rather fancied fucking her like that. Michiko looked at the trio on the wide bed. Jim reached out and pulled her to him by her lapels. Phyllis's eyes widened just as the first tremors of Jim's come coated her tongue. She tried to withdraw, then tried to clench her teeth on the pulsing object in her mouth. But Jim held her jaws, while extricating himself. Finally succeeding and swearing, his red erect cock continued pulsing dribblets of come into the air. He gasped and Phyllis glared at him. Andy was laughing hysterically behind her, his cock shrinking with laughter. Only Michiko looked on in interest and puzzlement. She touched the milky fluid with a curious forefinger, then grasped Jim's cock.

"It is so beautiful," said the young policewoman softly. Jim reached for her gratefully. Andy collapsed on the *futon,* still shuddering with laughter. Phyllis lost some of her outrage, as she spat the residue of Jim's come out of her mouth. "What did she say, the copper?" she demanded.

"She says Jim's come is beautiful," Andy mistranslated.

"Then she should suck it up!" the blonde snapped.

Andy translated back to Michiko.

"Of course I would do that," Michiko said. "If it gives Suzuki-san pleasure, why not?"

"You mean you'd let a man fuck your mouth? You've actually done that?" asked the heavy girl.

"I've never done that. But I would do it if Suzuki-san wished. After all, it is part of him."

"Go on. I don't believe all that," Phyllis said. "The stuff is awful."

"I think at the moment it's an academic question," said Jim. "I'm all finished for now." Andy echoed his words in Japanese for Michiko's benefit.

She reached for his flaccid cock and stroked it, then bent and kissed it lightly. "It will soon recover."

"Why not try the other one then," Phyllis said curiously.

Andy smiled and bowed.

"I will do all three of you," Michiko answered. "If you will do the same."

Phyllis eyed her with suspicion. "I'm not a lez," she said.

"A woman must please her lovers. And I am sure Suzuki-san and Andy-san would want to be pleased." She slipped forward and began sucking at Andy's half-erect cock. Jim helped her slip out of her uniform and Phyllis could see she had a smooth muscular body. Tiny brown tits were not a patch on her own, which made her feel better. But the Japanese girl was obviously enjoying her work, hollowing her cheeks hungrily in an effort to extract Andy's honey. Phyllis bent and watched the action from close up. Michiko glanced at her out of the corner of her eyes and smiled through her mouthful. She reached for the blonde's head and brought her closer. On the other side Jim watched the action too. Michiko started moving her mouth up and down the length of the shaft.

"I never taught her that," Jim said. "She's a natural."

CHAPTER 17:
The nut tree woman

Teruko Uabashi dithered in front of the apartment building for a full half-hour before screwing up her courage to enter. She knew that if she did not find it in herself to apologize to Suzuki-san, there would be nothing left to her but death. She was so involved with her internal struggle that she paid no attention to the observer hidden by the angle of a nearby building.

Finally she scurried into the apartment building. She checked the names on the mail boxes and found SUZUKI along with another name MIDDLER. She wondered if that was his wife's name, and almost retreated. She rang the bell and was relieved to see Jim's face at the door. For a breath she didn't know what to say. All her rehearsed apologies disappeared in her panic. He stood there, impassively, watching her from the carpeted floor of the hall.

"Please forgive me. Please." she finally managed to stutter out.

Suzuki-san did not reply, and she screwed up her courage. "May I come in? Please?" there was a sob in her throat. "Please," she whispered. "I must explain . . ."

He moved aside and admitted her to the room. She cast a hurried look around, impressed by the affluence she saw. It was like the company president's Tokyo office. Even some of the prints were the same lurid swirl of purples that she did not care for. She knelt on the mats and he followed suit, offering her a flat *zabuton* cushion with perfect politeness.

She bowed to the *tatami* in front of him. Jim looked at her in anger and some disgust. He had masturbated himself in a fury after she had left him and ended their encounter. Moreover, she would have been a good pipeline into the working of the company, and could have helped his quest considerably. He was clearly angry.

"Get out," he sighed. "I can't stand the sight of you."

"No, please Suzuki-san. You must not do this to me."

She started crying, with long, racking sobs. Her shoulders heaved. The tears ran down her face, streaking her makeup.

"There is nothing I can do," she whimpered. "I want to die. My husband . . . my husband he does not want me. I am not fine like the young girls. I do not cook to his liking. My friend was insulted by me. My family have disowned me. . . . There is nothing for me to do. No one cares. You do not care for me. I want to die." She rocked back and forth in agony.

"I care, all right? I just don't want anything to do with you now. I'm too angry."

"You should punish me then. Hit me. Just do not send me away. . . ."

"I don't want to punish you. I'm just mad and disappointed, that's all. I want you to go."

"No!!"

She scrabbled on the floor grovelling before him, her hands before her in the deepest bow she could perform. She felt the leather belt around her waist catch in the folds of her stomach. With a quick motion she released the clasp, handed it to him, remembering that her husband's rages with her poor performance as a housekeeper or at work were always allayed by beating her. She looked earnestly into his angry face, then bowed down again, her face to the floor. Perhaps this act of abasement would quiet her conscience for the wrong she had done Suzuki-san. Perhaps he would be ready to accept her apology. Once he had beaten her, her husband had always calmed down and forgiven her, and sometimes listened to her apologies for whatever she had done or failed to do.

Jim looked at the leather strap doubtfully. Her skirt was stretched tight over her full buttocks and he could see that she was wearing a rubber corset. He shrugged. It probably wouldn't hurt too much, and if he did what she wanted maybe she would leave him alone.

He struck once. She quivered and a thin yelp emerged from her. He struck again and again, a rational portion of his mind trying to limit the strokes, but another leading him on. Finally he threw away the belt and leaped upon her. The blood was pounding in his head and there was an urgent pressure in his groin. He fumbled for the zipper at the back of her skirt and pulled the material down. The rubbery girdle came next, a garment Jim had always hated. Flowery underpants followed, and she was naked to his gaze. Her buttocks were a bright pink. A small tuft of black hair jutted between them. He passed his hand over each half moon and she shuddered at the contact. His hand rose involuntarily and smacked down. She quivered and gasped at the attack, but did not try to stop him. Instead, to his surprise, he heard her call "More, more Suzuki-san. Yes, please, more."

Caught in the frenzy, he smacked again and again. He passed a hand through the crack of her ass and was not surprised to find it wet. Exposing himself, he advanced on her, aiming the full tip of his manhood at the opening of her purse, and jabbed himself forward. His cock made its way into her wet interior. She leaned forward onto the table, grasping the edges. Jim rammed himself into her and she collapsed onto the table, bruising her breasts and crying.

He leaned forward and bit hard at her neck. He leaned back, and slapped her buttocks twice. She impaled herself strongly onto his cock. His shaft steamed into her, shuttling with heat and speed. The little table danced on the mats. He paused and slapped her again. She squeaked, but this time he thought he could see pleasure on her face. He withdrew and she half turned to him in surprise.

"Take it off!" he commanded hoarsely. Teruko jumped to her feet and stripped the rest of her clothes off.

"Spread your legs!"

She did so, not complaining even as he forced them wider. He struck two fingers up into her gaping cunt, then slapped her thighs rhythmically. She began breathing deeply and her stomach jerked uncontrollably. He pulled the fingers out of her cruelly and looked at her. She met his eyes for a moment, then lowered them.

"Lie down on the floor and raise your ass!"

She hurriedly obeyed and he raised her bottom higher, forcing her to support her back with her hands, her feet over her head.

Jim squatted over her and said "Look at what I am doing. Don't close your eyes!" He then slapped her prominent buttocks several more times for emphasis.

Her position was excruciatingly uncomfortable. He spread her ass further and looked down at her exposed cunt and rectum, then squatted over her. She saw his erect prick come downwards, and she could not stop from gasping as the delight from the silky rod made its way through her nerve endings. He lowered his weight and penetrated her until he was sunk in to his balls. Raising himself, he plunged down into her, again and again. White froth accumulated at the stretched entrance. She flushed with pleasure, her chin bent to her chest. He saw and smiled, then pulled out of her. She gaped at him, surprised, then felt the tip of his fleshy sword at a hole she thought was used only for other things.

Jim thought to humiliate her further. Unlike Andy, he was not particularly fond of buggery, but she wanted to be used, and he was in the mood to abuse her. He lowered himself, but slowly this time. She gave way, as grunts escaped from her clenched lips. When he was on her, resting completely inside, he could see the faint smile return to her lips. He jogged up and down, slowly at first, intent on not injuring her. But when he saw the smile increase, he knew there was nothing to fear, and set about procuring his own enjoyment.

Faster and faster he plunged into her. His thighs locked and he thrust uncontrollably, legs trembling. A gush of sperm travelled painfully down his bent rod and inundated her channel. He gripped her thighs tightly as his balls and cock pulsed into her bowels. As his orgasm subsided, he did not have the strength to raise himself, and they fell sideways together, Jim only barely conscious that Teruko was jerking in orgasm, her head flailing.

They lay together on the mat until Teruko tried to pull away. Jim restrained her and began exploring her with his hands. She allowed him complete freedom, not even trying to restrain him as his fingers again invaded her inflamed cunt and backside.

"Why did you have your boyfriend attack me?" he asked idly. Most of his anger had burned away in the fire of his lust.

"Boyfriend?" she asked, surprised. "I have no boyfriend." She thought guiltily of Matsuoka and wondered what had become of him.

"Oh no? Who was it that attacked me then, when I left you at Kabukicho?"

She looked at him without comprehension. "I do not know, Suzuki-san."

He described the man, and saw that she really did not know anything of the incident. "Maybe its someone from your office," he said.

"Why should they care about me? I am a nobody."

"You're a pretty girl. From the president to the office boy, they probably all want to get into your pants."

The thought had never occurred to her. "I am not pretty," she said. "You are making fun of me."

He slapped her breasts roughly and she quivered. "Stupid woman. You are a great fuck and look great and you cry to me about being miserable . . . I bet the president has already been in here." He dug his thumb viciously between her cunt lips. She squeaked but obediently opened her legs.

"No, really," she whispered. "No one has . . . I mean, certainly not the president. I've only seen him once or twice. . . ." Her voice sank as if she were speaking of some august personage. She seemed shocked at the idea of being desirable.

"But his office is right there," Jim pressed.

"He has an office, but he is rarely there. The company headquarters is in Yamanashi Prefecture, in Kiso. The president only keeps an office for when he is in Tokyo."

"Are you telling me the whole operation is merely a blind?"

"Oh no," she said. "Our company is only the daughter company of Clouds and Rain Corporation. Mr. Kitamura, the president, is a very busy man and Mr. Sato does all the work here."

He squeezed her breast roughly, then spread her legs and mounted her to hide his agitation. Moving in her was almost mechanical, and when she urged him to beat her breasts he did it almost distractedly, waking up from his daze only when she clutched his butt to her and urged him to pinch her ass. They came together, she enthusiastically, Jim only a shadow of himself. He was yet distracted as they dressed, almost ignoring her. She took his silence as normal.

"Do you forgive me?" she asked timidly at the door.

His hug and surprisingly warm mouth gave her the answer she needed. Down in the street she looked up, saw his face in the window and waved. He smiled and waved back. She walked down the street and the hidden watcher lurched from his hiding place and fell into step behind her. She spun around. Matsuoka-san was peering at her in the dusk. Her heart leaped as she suddenly realized how much she really felt for him.

Matsuoka was drunk. His clothes were shabbier than they had been before.

"What are you doing now, Matsuoka-san?" she asked timidly.

"No' working. Chust livin' offa ma savinsh . ." he mumbled. He was much drunker than she had thought.

"Wha' you doin' comin' out of that apartment?" He screwed up his eyes at the *apato biru* from which Teruko had emerged.

"I was just . . . Just helping one of the clients from the office . . ." Her hand touched her bottom which was still sore, though the relaxation and peace in the rest of her limbs was more than enough compensation.

He looked at her owlishly and tried to frown, but staggered.

"I must take you home . . . Please Matsuoka-san, let me get a cab."

"Can' afford," he admitted. Tears leaked from his eyes.

He slumped in his corner of the cab all the way through the city. In her confusion she had given her own address. Now, still not sure he would come in, she was nonetheless glad she had done so. There was something so pathetic about his silent sobbing.

He sat on the cushion she had laid out, his shoulders bent. Teruko fetched a warm washcloth and gently wiped his face.

He pushed the towel away and glared at her. "So, where di' you learn tha'? Eh? Been a bar girl, Eh?"

"No!" she said horrified. "You know that's not true!"

"Whoring with that other man, eh? Wouldn't do it wi' me!?"

"But Matsuoka-san . . But we did! Why, . . . why did you . . ." She meant to complete "walk out on me," but her nerve broke. He misunderstood, and the shame of the failure of his first encounter with sex overcame him again. His rage blazed up anew. He snatched the washcloth from her hand and slapped her face hard. "It's you, you bitch! You wouldn't have me. So I . . . so I. An' I quit my job 'cause of you." His voice broke and he expected her to scream or object, but she was looking at him with tears in her eyes.

"That's all right Matsuoka-san. I don't mind. I understand," she said.

"What do you understand, what?" he was screaming again, his open hand trembling with suppressed desire, unfocused anger and confusion.

"It's all right. You can hit me again. Do it if it will make you feel better."

It did not seem to him that her words were an apology. Rather she was issuing him some sort of invitation, but in his addled state he was unable to figure out for what.

She saw his confusion and the politeness, inbred since infancy, that stayed his hands. "Here," she said rather more sharply than she had intended. "Hit me, beat me if it will make you feel better." She grabbed one of his hands and smacked it against her breasts. The smack caused her nipple to grow hard.

He blinked at her and she released his hand, then unbuttoned her blouse and exposed her breasts in their nylon cups. Her nipples were taut with expectation.

His hand stretched out hesitantly, stroked one fabric-covered mound, and then he was handling them ferociously. He shook her from side to side and her hair swayed before her face. Her tiny mouth opened with shock and seeing the surprise on her face, he let go. She fell to one side, a hip in the air, lying sideways. Without moving she said "That's all right Matsuoka-san. It's fine, I understand."

Matsuoka felt there was something mocking about her statement.

"Understand? What is there to understand? You left me, you let me go!" he said, raging against himself and the opportunity he had lost.

"Hit me then," she groaned. "Hit me and make it better." She rolled over onto her stomach and her face was hidden by the mass of her dark hair. Her skirt had been rucked up slightly and he could see the backs of her thighs. They were pale and smooth, touched with a tinge of pink. He did not move and merely stared at the vision before him, but his hands twitched.

Without a word she fumbled behind her and raised her skirt. The fullness of her buttocks were exposed to him.

"You're not even as good as that foreigner," she goaded him.

Matsuoka leaped at her and straddled her hips. Breathing heavily he stared at the plump hillocks, bisected by the dark crack and covered by two layers of nylon. She heaved up under him and he forced his hips downwards. Feverishly, with one hand he undid his fly and his erect cock struggled free. The flat of his right hand rose and fell on the soft straining rump before him. She wriggled from side to side and he held on like a horseman, with his knees. His cock

swayed and jerked before his eyes. Between slaps he pulled
down her panties and hose and exposed the warm full flesh.
He alternated, slapping first one and then the other mound
until they both glowed. At the same time he invaded her inner
parts with his left hand. He dipped a finger into the long
crack and felt along until he could touch the crinkled button
of her anus. Then lower down he felt the back of her female
slit and the beginning of its hairy guardian. In his excitement
he forgot to slap and a twist of her body almost unseated him.
He wondered if the wetness between her legs was due to her
own excitement or to the leavings of the *gaijin* whom she
practically admitted had had her.

Teruko tried to roll over. He slapped her several times to
control her twisting, but it only increased as the pain translated into passion. He was almost off her when she rose with
a sudden jerk, bracing her knees apart to buck him off. His
weight was momentarily off her, but then he was back, fully
on her back and ass. She fell prone to the floor again as his
hips forced her thighs apart. She yielded as his fingers dug
into her shoulder muscles. His fat cock was nudging the
entrance to her cunt. For a moment she feared he was about
to spear her behind, then he adjusted and the length of his
shaft was embedded firmly in her narrow wet channel.

"Hit my ass. Hard!" she pleaded in a whisper. All shame
was gone and she felt the need to express her own newly
awoken needs. Instead, he braced himself on her shoulders
and ground her chest into the *tatami* The abrasion of her
nipples against the matting was exquisite and she found herself moaning "Yes, yes," as he bent almost double and bit
her neck, her shoulders, her upper back.

All this time his cock hammered roughly into the depths of
her cunt. Matsuoka felt the heat of her ass cheeks as she
bucked against his belly. His cock sliding in and out of her
depths, ready to burst.

The climax, when it came, took both of them by surprise.
She was swept along with him as surge after surge of his seed
flooded her and fused her to him. He ground himself into her
mercilessly, clawing at her back and sides, clutching hungrily
at her breasts. His lust and need for her awoke a similar
response in her, and she let herself go, writhing in pleasure
and pain against the mats, enjoying the mixture of ecstasy
that washed away all her fears and guilt. They gradually
descended from the heights, their bodies still twitching in
sympathy. They lay still for a while, both knowing that a
false word or move could finish both of them, while the right
response would open an entire new life.

The excitement and the delight she gave him did not allow
Matsuoka's erection to fade. His cock softened somewhat as
he lay on her. But without withdrawing he leaned back and
clawed at her full ass. She looked over her shoulder and
smiled. They thrashed around again until she found herself
riding him, his stiff cock poking up into her interior. He
clawed with all ten fingers at the breasts that rose before him
and pulled her down onto his chest, then raised her and bent
his head. For a brief moment he licked one tumescent nipple,
then deliberately bit down on the inviting morsel of brown
flesh. She howled painfully, but did not attempt to pull away.

Locked together, mouth to mouth, penis in delighted vagina, they passed into a happy daze.

CHAPTER 18:
The widow's tale

"Gomen kudasai," Andy called out as he entered the store. "Excuse me for disturbing you!" There was a muffled shout from the rear. The shop itself was dark, darker than the evening outside, lit only by gloomy, dusty light bulbs that shed yellow light on the shelves of crockery. The shop was obviously not doing well. The glass door that separated the living quarters from the store slid open.

The woman looked at Andy inquiringly. "Yes? What can I do for you?"

Andy allowed himself a long stare. She was smooth skinned and rather plump. Her hair was heaped on her head and curls floated like the petals of a reddish brown flower. Her white blouse was not fully done up and he could see the top of an under-dress. She rose and stepped down onto the floor of the shop. "Yes?" she repeated, while one hand adjusted her skirt.

Andy wondered what she had been doing. Had she been at the toilet? Entertaining her husband? A lover? or merely taking her ease on the mat?

"I . . . that is, I wonder if I could speak to your husband? Mr. Hachimura is in?"

"I'm afraid not," she said pleasantly. "I am afraid he has passed away."

"I am so sorry," Andy mumbled. "Did he pass away a long while ago? I wanted to ask him some questions. About a man he knew."

"I am afraid it was quite a while ago. I don't know much about his affairs . . ." She waited for him to go.

Andy wondered again about what she had been doing. In his mind's eye he could see her spread out, her rich full figure supine on the mat or on some bedding. His penis responded immediately. The idea of a lover emerged again, and his pants bulged before him into a tent. She was still looking at him expectantly, waiting for him to leave. He backed away nervously. The relative darkness of the shop might obscure the large bulge in his pants. If he turned to go, the profile of his pants might cause her to call the police, he thought. Or not.

He turned to go. "One moment, sir," she said suddenly. Her voice was huskier somehow. As he turned to face her, he saw that her eyes were aimed directly at his crotch. "Perhaps I can help you?" she said politely, through a slight tremor. "Perhaps you would care to come up?" She beckoned hospitably at the house behind her. "My late husband might have left some papers. . . ."

He stepped out of his shoes and onto his knees on the mat. The erection was painful now, constricted by his pants. She hastily slid the door shut. He was grateful that the upper half was glass, the lower wood: whatever she planned would not be visible from the street.

She licked her lips for a moment, searching his face which he tried to keep as impassive as possible. Then her eyes dropped to the perceptible bulge in his pants. Her hand followed. He sat quietly, hands on his knees, not wanting to frighten away the exploring palm.

In a swift movement she reached for the zipper and undid his fly, then lowered his underpants. His penis rose forth, broad purple head shining.

"It is so beautiful," she breathed, then leaned forward from her knees and sucked the entire head into her soft mouth. It burned like a furnace. Her swift tongue explored the entire head, then her mouth withdrew slowly and she sat up. She licked her lips, savoring the taste, then rose quickly to her feet.

"Don't move please," she begged. She hastily stepped down onto the shop floor into her slippers, then moved rapidly about the small shop. The blinds were lowered and the doors locked. She was soon back with him. She faced him, a bit shyer then before, though the sight of his erection seemed to restore her randiness and allow her to overcome any last reluctance.

Andy slid his hands onto her knees beneath her skirt. The nylon slid scratchily under his palms. Her eyes closed to slits.

"It's been so long. So long."

She fell sideways and he half fell, half was pulled onto her as she clutched him to her breast. His hands sought the zipper in her skirt as she fumbled with his cock.

"One moment," she panted as they lay entangled. She stood up and rapidly stripped. Andy did the same and they examined one another for a brief moment before reaching for the target of their desire.

Mrs. Hachimura had a full chunky body. The signs of age were noticeable in the folds at her belly and the flabbiness of her breasts. But her skin was clear and smooth, dappled slightly as some Japanese women's skins are. The furry patch between her legs was tiny, barely covering the lips that pouted forward between her thighs. Andy reached for her and hooked his forefingers into the depths of her cunt. She grunted and pulled him to her by the most convenient handle. They sank down onto the mat, their bodies glued together. She spread her legs and urged him inside her and Andy's hips began pumping rapidly at her as she muttered and nibbled at his ear. Her fingers stroked his back, dipped between the cheeks of his rear, fondled his bag of stones from behind. He pounded her ass forcefully into the *tatami* and the ancient floorboards groaned with each thrust. The woman stiffened and pulled him to her, forcing more of his cock into her hungry chasm. Andy wriggled, raising his torso and legs until his full weight was concentrated on his hips and transmitted to her aroused clitoris. She trembled again and her cunt grew wetter with the pleasure of his cock, the first one she had had for over a year.

With an effort she rolled him over and impaled herself even more deeply onto him. She could feel the tip of the male shaft nudging at her cervix and grunted with satisfaction. He played with her breasts and explored her muscular body. As long as she controlled and forced the depth of the penetration, she was not concerned about anything else. Finally she raised her head and groaned deeply, matching the sounds of the floorboards beneath them. Her head rose higher and she stared blindly at the dark ceiling. Her cunt contracted strongly, in the cadence her husband had insisted on, and which had become second nature to her. She felt, though dimly, the spurt of semen from the man under her, more aware of the deeper penetration as the man arched his back in his own orgasm.

She looked down as the initial waves subsided. She was almost surprised to notice finally that he was a *gaijin*, then smiled at him as his panting subsided. His face relaxed, appeared older, and a ghostly image floated into her mind. The image of someone she had seen before.

She laid herself flat on him and examined his face more closely. Aware of something going on, Andy bore her weight without motion. Mrs. Hachimura sucked in some air through her teeth, and muttered something to herself. She shook her head in a Japanese gesture expressing doubt, mumbled some more, then slipped reluctantly off his cock. She groped behind her for some cover, found her blouse and put it on, then padded into another room without a backwards glance. Andy watched her muscular buttocks disappear, wondering what she had seen. He heard the sound of drawers being pulled out and replaced. Silently he stepped to the *fusuma* sliding door that separated the two rooms. Mrs. Hachimura was crouched before a waist high antique lacquered travelling chest, with drawers of various sizes. She was methodically searching their contents, muttering to herself the while. Finally she gave a cry of triumph and pulled out a plain flat wooden box. It was crammed with documents and photographs. She hurriedly searched through it and produced a photograph. Looking over her shoulder she saw Andy.

"Look at this, please!" Sudden embarrassment overtook her, and Andy realized that she did not even know his name. But the embarrassment passed with the sight of the photograph. She held it out to him, unconscious of their nudity. He examined it silently. It was an old black and white grainy photograph of a group of men and women. They were posed formally, in a group portrait. Two of them in the front row held a banner declaring "THE SUMMER OUTING OF THE CLOUDS AND RAIN COMPANY." She pointed with a finger. "There, that one is my husband." He was dressed in shirt sleeves and wore the peaked cap some drivers still affected in Tokyo. "There, there's the boss." A bespectacled individual, rather taller than the other Japanese, peered anxiously into the camera. Beside him stood another man. A dark non-Japanese. The plump face was familiar from the photograph Sissy had supplied. Leonard Fine. Andy's father.

"His name's Leonard Fine, right? Mine is different. I

never met him, and I'm called by my adoptive name, Andy Middler." She nodded without reacting. Adoption is common in Japan.

"Where was this taken?" Andy asked.

"Somewhere in Kiso," Mrs. Hachimura answered. "The company still exists. It was taken in the late fifties. My husband left to start his own business, though his relationship with his employer was very good. He even came to the funeral. Mr. Kitamura is a very good man," she said.

"Mr. Kitamura?" Andy's blood ran cold. "Kitamura Dansuke, is it?"

"Yes," she said, turning. "Do you know him? Of course, you must. The other man, your father. I've also met him, years ago. He is a great friend of Kitamura-*sacho*." She blushed slightly and Andy could not help but wonder what their relationship had been. She looked downwards in confusion and squatted to return the boxes and bundles to the open drawer. Andy wanted to question her more about the company, about the mysterious Mr. Kitamura and about his father, but he knew that she had turned away with a reason, and that pushing too hard would do him no good. He looked down at her and at the fine plump ass that stuck out from under her shirt tail. His cock twitched, reminding him that there were ways to tie her to him.

Andy squatted behind her and his palms slid down her full round buttocks. The crack between them was dark and smooth. He clutched at the prominent lips that were wet with his sperm with one hand, while fisting his root with the other. Her hands stopped their task of arranging the drawer and he nuzzled his sticky semi-soft cock at the entrance to her cunt. The tip of the head slipped in and the warmth and wetness roused it the rest of the way. She held on to the open drawer with her hands while he inserted his cock into her, then she leaned back to make it penetrate deeper. He could barely move in the position and she did most of the work, bouncing lightly on his lap. He mouthed and nibbled at her nape and she gratefully arched her neck while swivelling her buttocks luxuriously against his belly.

They fell into dreamy slow motion, almost the only movements being those of her hips swivelling against his. He supported her ass easily with his hands, not bothering to touch her elsewhere. The speed of her movements increased until they were both panting and the ancient *tansu* rattled with the grip of her hands on its drawer. The rush of his sperm inundated her insides and she groaned with disappointment, grinding her ass heavily against him, imprisoning his traitorous cock inside her. She tried to clench her muscles to squeeze her own pleasure out but was unsuccessful. One of her hands dipped to her cunt and she masturbated herself rapidly to a climax. Andy helped as best he could by trying to force his hips into her, and keeping his reluctant cock erect by sheer willpower. At last she gave a shrill cry and he could feel her insides spasm with pleasure. She fell against him, and he held her tightly.

Drinking tea, he smiled at her tentatively and said "We should do it again."

She smiled back "But no more here. My neighbors would talk. Where do you live?"

Andy wrote down his address and she looked at him thoughtfully.

"Next time we will do it properly. You were too quick," she said critically.

Andy bowed in embarrassed acknowledgement.

"That is all right, Andy-san. I will teach you how to please a woman. My husband was very demanding." She stroked his hand consolingly.

"Can you tell me anything more about the people in the picture? Where I can find them?"

"I never worked for the company," Hachimura admitted. "I've only met the people concerned . . . ." She floundered in confusion which Andy paid no attention to. ". . . in other circumstances, such as when they visited Tokyo. But maybe I can find out for you?"

"Would you please?" Andy begged. "I have never met either of them . . ."

They sipped their tea and talked about her life and his. She was curious about every aspect, exclaiming in wonder about his life in America, about his work, talking a little about herself and the difficulties of being a single woman in a male-oriented society. She was not a businesswoman and the shop had run downhill after her husband had died. She was thinking of selling out and going to join her married daughter in Niigata, but the cold and lack of friends deterred her.

Finally Andy took his leave and stepped down off the *tatami* house platform and into his tooled leather boots.

"I'll get the information for you if I can, Middlaa-san." she promised. "Maybe tomorrow."

The lights of Tokyo glittered around him as he made his way back home, deep in thought.

CHAPTER 19:
Spring again

Andy sleepily groped for the telephone, cursing mildly. He could hear Jim tapping away at his keyboard in the other room.

"Yes?" he grunted ungraciously into the phone.

"Andy honey? Don't you recognize me?"

He rolled over onto his back, his mind fogged for a moment, and then the voice acquired a face. "May! May McCormick! I thought you had gone back to the US?"

"I have and I'm back again. We flew into Osaka and I convinced Harry that Osaka is even worse than Tokyo for me and came here to wait for him." Her voice grew tentative "Is there . . I mean . . ."

"How would you like to come to our apartment?" he asked. "Jim would be delighted at an excuse to stop working."

She laughed. "And what about you?"

"Very busy," he said huskily. "I'm lying in bed naked and stroking an enormous erection. How does that grab you?"

There was a catch in her voice when she answered.

"It grabs me a lot. So much in fact that I don't want you to move. I'll grab a cab until I can grab you.'' The phone clicked off.

"It's for me, I'll get it!" Andy yelled as the doorbell rang. May stood there, packages in her hands. Her hair had been recently done and it framed her large plump face with the perfection only a professional could achieve. She was dressed in an ankle length black coat that was held closed against the early spring cold. He drew her inside, kissed her red-painted lips, and motioned her to silence, a conspiratorial grin on his face.

"Jim doesn't know," he whispered. "I want you to surprise him. I've told him often enough that when he starts working on those damn computers of his he becomes dead to the world." She was still standing on the *genkan,* the street-shoes level of the apartment. He stooped to help her out of her high heels and she supported herself by holding onto his head. Deciding to surprise her, he rose slowly inside her coat, his lips trailing up her bare legs. She giggled softly and he found that she had a surprise for him as well. Under the warm thick coat she was totally naked.

His lips brushed against the lush hairs of her bush and he rose higher against the solid curve of her belly. She unbuttoned the coat from the bottom up as he rose, until they were both encased in the black tent, his rigid cock butting against her belly, her tits pressed hard against his chest.

Andy slipped his tongue between her lips and she sucked on it, playing a counter with her tongue. He grasped her buttocks firmly and squeezed. She let out a contented sigh.

"You know," he said conversationally, "I'm going to fuck that ass of yours. I've never had one like it."

"So fat?" she said with a trace of asperity.

"So luxurious and feminine and inviting," he said, burying his hands into the tense mounds as he buried his lips in her hair.

"I've never done that," she whispered into his ear, her hands scratching on his bare back. "But if you want . . . Only first, I've had fantasies about you both for the past months. For once Japan has been something I've looked forward to."

"Of course," Andy said with a smile. "Now listen, he's sitting there, his back to the door. He's wearing sweatpants which can be pulled down easily . . . No, I have a better idea." He whispered into her ear and she agreed, giggling.

Jim was staring at the computer screen. His hands were resting motionless in his lap. He was watching the monitor sequence on the screen alertly, though no one would have been able to tell from the glazed look in his eyes. The consequences of each string of numbers were as clear to him as a navigator's map. He mulled over alternatives to the paths he had created. The screen was suddenly cut off from his vision and two incredibly soft, heavy clouds covered his face and were rubbed into his eyes. He tried to push them away but found that his hands were imprisoned. For a long moment he was utterly disoriented. Something in his cortex was triggered by the smell and tactile sensation of the objects blocking his vision. Messages travelled from his spine to his mouth and down to his loins. His lips and tongue nipped and sucked at the two mounds to the sound of muted squealing while his cock stirred and began to engorge. Slowly his conscious mind uncoupled from its interlock with the machine and rational memory stirred. He stopped struggling, and his hands began exploring the soft thigh flesh that enveloped his hands and forced his lap back into the chair. He nuzzled at the fat breasts before his face, and the sensation rapidly translated into something familiar.

"May?" he mumbled indistinctly. Then louder "May!" and he bit at one of the breasts which was jerked back. She stared down at him, laughing joyfully, then looked past his shoulder. "It took him time, but he did remember."

"I remembered immediately," Jim said indignantly. "Only it took me some time to react. I was busy with a problem."

Andy and May laughed. She slipped off his lap and pulled him to his feet. He admired the jiggly fullness of her as she pulled his pants down and kissed his semi-erect penis. He stripped off the rest of his clothes and stood naked before her. His room was in its usual disorder. Clothes and books were piled everywhere, and since he had started work on the computer in the early morning, he had not bothered to put away the *futon* sleeping quilts.

May had time to look around for a few seconds before the two men reached for her full body. They pushed her down, giggling with protests, onto Jim's *futon*. The three of them rolled about, May pretending to struggle. She felt their firm warm skins and her fingers touched and fondled every inch of them she could. This was the second time in a rather staid life that she had let herself go. This was less like lust, more like innocent puppy play, notwithstanding the stiff cocks and her own aching breasts.

Her desire came to her more strongly. Jim was doubled up, nibbling one of her feet. Andy was scratching her back lightly while his penis jerked at the mound of her belly. She pushed them off, still smiling though more serious now, and sat up. Her breasts spread wide and jounced on her chest. Jim eyed them appreciatively, remembering her fondness for them. She saw his gaze and cupped both heavy breasts. Then without a word, she raised each one in turn and sucked the nipple, covering as much of the tit as she could with licks of her long pink tongue. The two men looked on entranced, then moved toward her on their knees.

"Do you know what I really like?" she asked seriously.

"No, tell us," said Jim as his erection threatened from the side.

"I like my tits fucked," she said glancing up at them in anticipation. "Not just between them. All over. I've fantasized about that all my life. I've had some lovers besides Harry; I don't think he keeps himself for me when he's away on his business. But I've never felt as free as I have with you two. There's a lot of things I haven't done with a man, and which I'm ready to try." She gave Andy a shy, meaningful look as she said that. "But there's one thing I want, and have wanted for myself, ever since my tits started growing seriously. I want a man to love them and fuck them as they should be."

"I'd rather have your mouth," said Jim, leering comically.

"You can have that too," she said composedly. "Just now though, do what *I* want. We can please each of us in turn."

They looked at one another and grinned. They shuffled forward in concert and started rubbing the tips of their cocks against her tits. She cupped the full bags up for them and they reciprocated by pulling at the breasts with their hands and stabbing into the yielding springy prominences with their cocks. Soon, the jerking of their hips came in spasms and their breathing came in heavy gasps. At first May followed the action curiously, directing portions of her breasts to each of the cocks on either side of her. But as her reality and imagination fused, she lost all track of conscious thoughts, responding instinctively to the drive of her body. Not noticing, she began moaning in time with the men's thrusts. Her body arched as she tried to force as much of her aching breasts as she could against the silky poles. They triphammered against her skin and against her taut nipples. She started rolling her shoulders and trying to force the cocks deeper into her. For a moment rationality returned and she looked up into the man's faces, so different and yet so similar. They were not looking at her anymore. Their eyes were glazed and the throbbing of their shafts told her that momentarily they would spurt upon her jugs with their cream. They stiffened and ground into her without mercy. She gave one last wailing cry and pulled them roughly to her. Streams and gobs of milky fluid splattered against her breasts and ran down her sides. At the touch of the warm fluid and the uncontrollable jerking of the male members against her, she felt strings of delight run down from her breasts to a glowing fire in her belly. She arched her hips one more time as her orgasm struck, then fell back onto the thick quilt, pulling both male members and their bodies along with her into a warm suffocating heap.

They squirmed around after a while until she found her head pillowed on the men's thighs. They idly stroked her hair and she kissed each strong-smelling, softening cock in turn, then slipped them into her mouth and licked off the remainder of the come.

Glancing down she saw her breasts shiny with puddles and spots of the male residue. Idly she rubbed them into her breasts and was rewarded with a tiny flicker of mini-climax. She shuddered and clutched the two men to her tightly.

The doorbell rang, breaking into their silent enjoyment.

"What if we stay as we are and all of us go and answer?" May said.

The two men looked in the direction of the hall, and the thought tickled their fancy. But reality and their reason prevailed.

"No, we'll just ignore it," they said together.

The ringing persisted and Andy stopped ramming her full tits. "I'll go and see . . ."

He came back seconds later and motioned to Jim to join him. Reluctantly the *nisei* abandoned May's arms and joined his brother.

"Its Mrs. Hachimura, the woman from the shop in Kita-ku.

She knows someone's here. We can't afford to alienate her! She promised me some answers and I'd lose her as a source of information.''

"I'll answer the door and tell her you're not here."

Andy returned to Jim's bedroom and pulled May down on the *futon*. "I'm going to fuck your mouth," he growled. The action would keep her quiet while Jim got rid of Hachimura.

Hachimura was surprised to see a Japanese answer the door, but the face was remarkably familiar. "Is Middler-san here please?"

"No," said Jim. "I'm afraid he's out."

At that moment May pulled back from Andy's cock and said "That is one great COCK." She laughed hoarsely. Hachimura's eye caught the sight of Andy's boots.

"He is here, ne?" Her Japanese assumed more of the fiery tones of her childhood Kyushu and she pushed in, past Jim who stood bemused in his robe at the doorway. He shut the door and followed her ample form.

She stood facing the couple on the bed, arms akimbo. She was gathering air for what seemed to be a lengthy and loud denunciation of the pair before her. Andy was caught open mouthed, one hand on May's lips, the other squeezing her ample breast. May, upon sighting a rival, was filling her own lungs, pink nipples rising, apparently about to contribute to the noise.

As one, Andy and Jim acted to save themselves. Jim bent, slid his hands up Hachimura's smooth legs and with one motion pushed her onto the bed and pulled off her underthings. Andy pulled the pillow out from behind May causing her to fall back, and eeled between her legs while with one hand he helped hold Hachimura down. Before Hachimura could formulate a counterattack, Jim had spread her legs and his rampant cock was searching the entrance to her plump cunt. Both female orifices were filled at the same time, and each of the two women gave a gratified grunt as the weight of a young man came down upon her.

Jim started pumping hard into the Japanese woman. She reached for her skirt pulling it up between their bodies and exposing more of herself to his hands. Jim placed his hands flat on her buttocks and massaged the full muscular buns. She wriggled appreciatively.

"I am Andy's brother. My name is Jim," he whispered in her ear.

"Ah . . . ah . . . Atsuko Hachimura. *Hajimemashite*." She added the formal phrase and laughed as raucously as he. He pulled out of her and she rolled over and spread her legs. Atsuko turned her head and watched with interest as Andy mounted May and plugged into her anew. May resisted for a second, conscious of the insult she thought she felt. Then the delicious feel of his cock in her waiting cunt and the touch of his hands and mouth on her full breasts got to her and she surrendered to the pleasure of the fuck. Her gaze went past her shoulder and lit on the short Japanese woman who was staring at her and her lover. The woman had reddish hair, obviously a common commercial dye and perm job. She seemed about the same age as May, though her skin had the smoothness of someone much younger. Atsuko was more muscular, her skin finer, but less rounded than May. May's breasts, flattened somewhat by her position and by Andy's probing palms, still towered higher than Atsuko's ever had, even before the inevitable sag of middle age. Both of their thighs were plump and full, May's a trifle thicker, Atsuko's a trifle smoother. As the motions of the men in them began to bring about tremors in their insides, the sight of each other drove both women to greater efforts, each one convinced she could outlove the other.

"Shall we change?" Jim said abruptly amidst the wordless sounds of sex.

Andy quickly slipped out of May and moved over to Atsuko's side.

"Hey," May complained. "What do you think you're doing? Don't I have a say in this?"

"What is she saying?" Atsuko said in Japanese as she spread her legs to facilitate Andy's entry. Andy translated and Atsuko snorted in derision. "I can pleasure both of you myself, if she's not up to it."

Jim translated for May who glowered at her rival. "If that yellow bitch thinks she can take my men away from me . ."

Jim pinched her nipple and she yelped. "Watch it, white woman. *I*'m yellow too, and for all we know, Andy as well."

"I'm sorry honey." She was instantly contrite, reaching to enfold him again and urging him on by jogging her hips. Andy translated for Atsuko.

"*Her* men? I could take them away from her any time." Her Kyushu accent, harsh and rough became a burr.

"Oh yeah, honey? You and your weightlifter figure?"

The two men grinned at one another, contenting themselves with word for word translations as they lay above the scrapping women.

"That bitch is looking for a fight," May fumed. Jim, lying above her, his cock dipping into her, was almost ignored.

"That woman must have some Korean blood in her," snapped Atsuko. "Constantly quarreling and not knowing her place . . . She knows I'm better than her, at any rate."

"Oh yeah?" May rose, pushing Jim off her and glared at her rival. "Better? How?"

"I'll bet I can please men better than you," said Atsuko. Her lips firmed in challenge. "I'll show you."

"All you can do, you greedy old bag, is cause them to spurt into you. Any woman could do that," May snapped back, all her reserve gone. The two men, passive for once, served only to translate the exchanges. The fierceness of the two claimants was so strong it did not occur to either of them to modify and pacify the exchanges they translated.

"Is that so?" some of the calm had returned to Atsuko's face. "No. I will pleasure both of them, fully. And myself."

May smiled sweetly "You do that, baby."

Atsuko positioned the men side by side. She knelt over their legs, then applied her mouth to both erect cocks. At first she alternated between them, then she brought both cocks together and sucked the tips simultaneously. She played with the ball sacks, comparing their weight and feel. Her furry cunt rubbed against the men's shins and they assisted her by raising their knees against the soft sopping flesh and hairs. Jim and Andy watched her mouth and hands bobbing over them. She was too far to touch properly, and Jim reached for May instead. She evaded his grasp sulkily, but the sight and sound of her rival pleasing both her men riveted her gaze. As the action grew faster she allowed herself to be pulled into the fun until her own legs were spread as pillows for the two male heads while their fingers played idly with the lips of her cunt. Atsuko cautioned her not to interfere, and May subsided somewhat, though the demand in her loins grew with every movement of the digits manipulating her sex.

Atsuko felt the heat rising in the balls she was handling, and raised her torso. She slid forward on Jim and poised herself over his erection, then lowered herself, holding open the lips of her cunt to afford the men a better view of the descent. She jogged herself on the magnificent member until she saw that Andy was getting restless.

"Get behind me Andy-san," she instructed hoarsely.

Andy grinned and moved to kneel behind her. He parted her buttocks and examined the ass hole with satisfaction. The tiny bud was slightly open, as if beckoning him inside. Atsuko smiled at him over her full smooth shoulder and held his shaft tightly with one fist. "You will have to make an effort, so please let me guide you."

Andy grinned. "I have done this before," he said.

She shook her head negatively, then ordered May through Jim to come around to her behind and observe the process. She leaned forward and guided Andy's rampant cock to her cunt hole, even though already occupied by Jim's thick pole. Andy, leaning back to observe, grinned with pleasure as she aimed the tip of his erection into her cunt. He pushed forward gently, then harder, as he felt the resistance of the vaginal muscles to the insertion.

Atsuko abandoned her attempts to guide him and braced herself over Jim's form. "Push harder," she grunted. Andy complied and felt his cock slide the length of Jim's shaft and into her warm cavern. Soon he was moving furiously into her, his hands slapping her full buttocks and urged on by her cries. May watched the action with amazement.

Half an hour later May was looking at the three figures before her with open-mouthed admiration. The two young men were panting heavily and somewhat dazedly. They reflexively stroked Atsuko's heaving flanks and she smiled in triumph at her rival. The men's cocks, still painfully erect, glistened with their juices. Seeing May's incredulous expression mollified the Japanese woman. "Yes?" she asked, the only English word she knew.

May nodded silently.

Atsuko smiled at her and May tentatively smiled back.

"Would you like to try? I will teach you . . ." She looked carefully at May. The pink soft body had revolted her at first, but now that she had won, she saw its good points and noted it was not assimilar to her own. Except, of course for the large bust, which she envied. She wondered what the weight felt like, and whether May found the large breasts a bother. Or only a pleasure and a lure.

May nodded convulsively, then said "I will try that, but
. . . but there are things I've never tried. . . . But I'll do
what you wanted!" She blushed slightly and glanced nervously at Andy's cock. Her breathing quickened.

Andy, who had been translating, said slowly in English "I
think I remember. Are you sure you want to try it? You're a
virgin, *there* I mean . . ." He wondered why, after all they
had done, he felt constrained by May's obvious discomfort to
speak in euphemisms.

"I'll do it," May said emphatically. "I want you. Its new
and I'm ready for it." She stroked her breasts and started
moving on her seat.

"What is she saying?" Atsuko demanded.

"I think," said Jim in Japanese, "that there are things she
has never done before, and that she is ready to try now."

"What?" Atsuko demanded.

The tone, if not the meaning of the single word was clear
to May. She raised herself to her knees and half turned,
patting her ass softly.

"Is that all?" Atsuko exclaimed. "It is wonderful. Tell her
that. It is very pleasing to many men, slightly forbidden and
naughty. My husband . . . and . . . . and," she groped with
embarrassment for words, "and someone else enjoyed it and
taught me to do it for them. Why should Mayu-chan be
embarrassed? I will teach her."

The use of the diminutive, used between intimate female
friends startled the two men. Their gazes brightened. They
looked on with interest as Atsuko arranged May comfortably
on a pile of cushions. The full white buttocks, smooth and
slightly dimpled stood uppermost. May looked over her shoulder, apprehension mixed with anticipation on her face. Atsuko
stroked the upturned buns, then led Andy and Jim to either
side. Each of them squeezed a hanging breast and May
squeaked thankfully. Atsuko's brown hands separated the two

white half moons and she allowed the men to look, and then to trace the length of the deep valley, exploring it with their fingers. Its bottom was hidden by dark curly moss, almost wiry luxuriant growth that complemented May's pouting cunt lips. Higher up they could examine the tiny clenched bud, the virginity that May was now anxious to lose.

Atsuko's brown finger probed lightly at the closed hole, wiggling in tiny circles until it opened reluctantly and allowed the digit in. Atsuko smiled at May's upturned face and impulsively leaned forward and kissed one upraised bun. The men watched in fascination as the finger pierced the hole again, enlarging and soothing it. Atsuko's finger withdrew and she brought the men's hands to the opening. She held the buttocks apart while frigging May's cunt with one finger. May responded by arching her back and pushing her ass backwards. The two men applied a finger each to the hole and gently inserted them against the push of the muscle.

May felt the two masculine digits examining her rear. Their motions were clinical at first, as if she were on a doctor's examination table. But gradually she began to feel the beginning of an unfamiliar sensation as the nerves in her breasts and pussy shot messages of pleasure up her spine, and her body learned to accept the pleasure from her anus as a legitimate one. She moved now with the tide aroused by the hands. Atsuko abandoned the group and May was distressed. The Japanese woman returned, and May found herself smiling at her former rival.

Atsuko anointed the tiny bud with cold cream from her purse and motioned one of the men forward. She positioned the tip of the stiff cock before the shiny bud, and pulled the shaft forward. The tip of the head started to enlarge the hole. The American woman grunted slightly and breathed through her mouth. The hole widened as Atsuko pulled at the shaft until the flanges of the head were about to disappear.

"Oh, it hurts," May gasped.

"It's nothing," Atsuko said firmly. "The pain is almost over." She removed her hand from the shaft and encouraged the man by slapping his buttocks. The other male face peered on with interest as the shaft sank to the hairs inside May's rear. Atsuko held him there motionless until May began moving back and forth by herself. The speed of her motions increased as she discovered that her muscles were relaxed enough to accept the intruder. She started shivering uncontrollably when a male mouth applied itself to one of her breasts and another nibbled and sucked at her back. Suddenly she found herself climaxing uncontrollably, from every hole and pore of her body as her rear channel flooded with the man's emission. She clenched her anal muscles tightly, not wanting to lose the wonderful meat, but it slipped out of her grasp, squirting out by the motion of the muscles with which she had hoped to retain it. The softened cock was immediately replaced by another, harder one, and May gratefully put her head back on the cushion and rocked to a second climax, as massive and as satisfying as the earlier one.

The four of them lay sprawled on the *futon*, entwined sleepily.

"I forgot," Atsuko said suddenly. "I came here with a message for you. Kitamura-san no longer opposes your efforts. He would be pleased to see you at his home."

Jim and Andy stared back at her dark eyes. "Is that all? Well, where is it?"

"In Kiso," she smiled at them.

"*Where* in Kiso?"

"Ah," she sucked air in between her teeth. "That the message did not say."

"What's this all about," May inquired.

Jim explained and May gasped and put a hand to her mouth. "I forgot too!" she said. "I have some presents for you both, but there's one I got from Harry that *is* relevant to you two." She rummaged among the shopping bags she had brought and said apologetically as she handed a small gift-wrapped package to each man "I am sorry Atsuko-chan. I have nothing to give you. In thanks." She touched the other woman's shoulder lightly.

"It does not matter," Atsuko smiled. "Maybe you will come to visit me some day?" There was a hidden promise in the words that May was anxious to fathom. But not here. In private, or perhaps just with Atsuko. Her fingers lingered briefly on the warm smooth skin, and withdrew.

"Ah! Here it is!" She withdrew a small bottle of perfume. The small vial was labelled simply TOUCH ME. Under it was a printed picture of a traditional Japanese mansion against the backdrop of a three-peaked mountain. "Harry said it was a sample. The company that sells it has a fantastic reputation, but yet they are not well known. They never sell under their own brand name. Anyway, what got me interested, aside from the incredible fragrance, is that Harry said the company was run by two men, a Japanese and a foreigner, who use their company villa as a logo."

Jim and Andy looked at one another speculatively, then reached together for the vial. It was manufactured by the Clouds and Rain Corporation. In Kiso.

"You know, Phyllis could be back any day now," Jim said thoughtfully as they peered out of the window at the clouds. May and Atsuko had both departed, walking in wordless amity towards tha Aoyama-dori road.

"You afraid she might cry rape?"

"No, I just can't stand spongers. You know brother, we have enough information to find those two. I think we should travel."

"Where? Kiso is large . . ."

"Look, its spring, the *sakura* are blooming, its time to think of some fun, and I haven't had a vacation the whole year. Let's travel."

They agreed.

END OF PART 1

PART 2: THE MASTERS OF CLOUDS AND RAIN

(BLUE MOON BOOKS

____ EVELINE/65001/$3.95
____ ''FRANK'' AND I/65442/$4.95
____ A MAN WITH A MAID/65003/$4.95
____ ROMANCE OF LUST BOOK I/65004/$3.95
____ SECRET TALENTS/65005/$3.95
____ THE BOUDOIR/65441/$4.95
____ DREAM BOAT/65007/$3.95
____ PLEASURE BOUND/65008/$3.95
____ LA VIE PARISIENNE/65009/$3.95
____ VENUS SCHOOL MISTRESS/65010/$3.95
____ SWEET DREAMS/65011/$3.95
____ SUBURBAN SOULS BOOK I/65012/$3.95
____ LOVE LESSONS/65013/$3.95
____ ROMANCE OF LUST BOOK II/65014/$3.95
____ WOMAN OF THE MOUNTAIN, WARRIORS OF
        THE TOWN/65015/$3.95
____ SUBURBAN SOULS BOOK II/65016/$3.95
____ THE OXFORD GIRL/65017/$4.50
____ BLUE TANGO/65018/$4.50
____ GREEN GIRLS/65019/$3.95
____ MISS HIGH HEELS/65020/$3.95
____ RUSSIAN ROULETTE: THE SOVIET ADVENTURES
        OF PROFESSOR SPENDER/65021/$4.50
____ IRONWOOD/65022/$4.95
____ THOMASINA/65023/$4.50
____ THE CALAMITIES OF JANE/65024/$3.95
____ AN ENGLISH EDUCATION/65025/$4.50
____ THE RITES OF SODOM: PROFESSOR SPENDER'S
        MIDDLE EASTERN TRIP/65026/$4.50
____ MY SECRET LIFE/65027/$9.95
____ DREAMS OF FAIR WOMEN/65028/$4.50
____ SABINE/65029/$4.50
____ THE TUTOR'S BRIDE/65444/$4.95
____ A WEEKEND VISIT/65031/$4.50
____ THE RECKONING/65032/$4.50
____ THE INTERRUPTED BOSTON/65443/$4.95
____ CAROUSEL/65034/$4.50
____ BELLE SAUVAGE/65035/$4.50
____ WOMEN OF GION/65036/$4.50
____ PEARLS OF THE ORIENT/65037/$4.50
____ THE CAPTIVE/65408/$4.50
____ BOMBAY BOUND/65405/$4.50
____ CHRYSANTHEMUM, ROSE, AND
        THE SAMURAI/65406/$4.50